twin time:
or, how death befell me

SEMIOTEXT(E) NATIVE AGENTS SERIES

Published by Semiotext(e)
2007 Wilshire Blvd., Suite 427, Los Angeles, CA 90057
www.semiotexte.com

Special thanks to Sarah Wang.

Cover Design by Liam Gillick
Cover Photography by Enrique Metinides "Adela Legeratta Rivas, struck by a Datsun, 1979" Courtesy of Blum & Poe Gallery, Los Angeles.

Back Cover Photography by George Porcari
Design by Hedi El Kholti

ISBN-10: 1-58435-048-2
ISBN-13: 978-1-58435-048-4
Distributed by The MIT Press, Cambridge, Mass. and London, England
Printed in the United States of America

twin time:
or, how death befell me

Veronica Gonzalez

For J and P

Contents

1:
Mara and the baker

(Mexico City, 1967)

One quick turn

The night was long. It was dark and the night was long. He was a man; she saw that now. And she a girl. She'd never ever dreamt that this could really happen. Like this. In a car, fleeing in the night. The darkness of the night. He was driving and she was staring out the window, silent, a girl, sixteen, who had never left her mother's side. It was like a dream; in fact she thinks she dreamt this once, a man she does not really know, does not feel anything for, his face unfamiliar, driving her, fast, away from her mother. And the landscape, in her dream it had changed quick several times, like it has here, now, changed several times in the past six hours, the big forests to the north of Mexico City—she'd never even known there were forests to the north of the city, they are forests, all those trees—and then dry almost desert when they came down, and now back to lush green as they began climbing out of the dry valley once again; and she was tired. In her dream she had been tired, head knocking into glass. He had not even stopped to eat. For he was driving with determination. And she was staring out the window, eyes big against the lack of light, head sifting like two kinds of sand what was once a dream and what was her life now, here, in this car.

They hadn't spoken since just after he'd started driving. And she would not look in his direction.

With her mother she could cry and scream and throw a fit and it meant nothing. Could cry and scream and scream, was just a way to let it out. Her mother would grab her up from a crumpled heap there on the bed, a mess of limbs there on the floor, and hug her. Tell her to be quiet, collect her and pat and pat and smooth her head.

What was she doing here, with this young man? She had said yes. Kind of. She knew him; kind of.

What she did know well was that he was different than anyone she'd ever met before. She knew this from the first time that she saw him and already there was something which told her she would get to know him well before too long. He was not handsome or at once smart and quick tongued, so it was not these typical things which had attracted her, but she could tell that he was different; and it must have been this that made her angry too, for she did feel angry: his differentness, her inability to know what he was all about. Can the same thing that attracts you make you angry? she wondered once or twice. And then she found out more about him and one of the things she found out was that he wanted to make things all the time; and this too was different. He had a little bakery already, a little shop all his own and it wasn't like other bakeries with their huge trays onto which you just piled and piled the heavy bread—he made really special things, delicate little sweets; and it was this that had brought her back, the specialness of his treats. She'd wandered in one day and had meandered around the small space, the light pouring in through plate glass windows, and it was a relief from the great big harshness of the street, the smell of warm cakes; and she saw him stare from where he stood behind his counter. She continued to peer into cases, the custard pies, not just flans, but pies with rose-water custard inside, and little lime tarts, a row of small purple cakes—and those impossibly fragile chocolate labels defining every treat, lavender essence this one read; and instead of the cinnamon and molasses cookies in the shape of piggies which every other bakery had, he had a whole farmyard: cows and chickens and a little licking cat. And then in a case right by where he stood was the chocolate and the marzipan; and she saw it there, the tiny little mouse made of chocolate with eyes of pink marzipan. And when she glanced up there he was still staring, and she decided that she would not like him right then though she could already tell by the way he shied away when she looked back, could tell he did like her.

And then she asked him for the mouse in a slow and measured voice and he stuttered as he asked her which one, though she had just told him, the mouse, and he awkwardly handed her that treat she had picked out. She smiled at him even though she didn't like him, only for an instant; her own smile a surprise to her, and then she ran out of the door. And then later on, that night in bed it made her angry, much more so than before, that he liked her. This was when she got really mad. Who did he think he was? Didn't he see that she was too pretty? That she had a mother who loved her and let her cry and throw fits? Who did that stuttering idiot baker think he was? She knew her eyes were hazel, and large, and that she shut them so slow with each blink. She knew what she could do with one of her slow looks; and who did he think he was? She had men chasing her and her mother loved her so much.

But she went back after a stroll through the park on her way home from school and again she looked through every case and this time she bought a lovely meringue, like a white cloud, and on top of it a little chocolate heart. And after a few more times of this going back he began to talk to her. And to her surprise his talking eased her anger so she began to talk back. And on this day she said she was on her way home from school, that she hated school and that some-times her mother did not make her go. Though she did not tell him that much of the time she and her mother just lay in bed when she was supposed to be at school. Or that if Mother were not at home to lie with, she would often just go to the cinema alone. And then the next time she went back her voice went proud as she told him about how much fun she had with her mother, how many friends her mother had, but after a short and confused pause her voice faltered and then softened and she added that even so her favorite thing was to go to movies and walk around the park all by herself. And then, on her now frequent visits she began to complain to him about things she had not even known were bothering her, about things she had not even known were problems at all. Her mother was always pressuring her. She had a friend who had a lot of money and was in love with Mara. And, well, Mara didn't love him back. He was old and she didn't even want to be around him, this old man, when she knew he loved her like that. And he stunk. And here *he* was, this baker, this sweets maker and he listened to her, listened so well that she did not even know what she was saying when she said it. So well, that it was only upon listening back to her own voice at night, in these late night I-can't-fall-asleep replays, that she knew things were problems at all. If she were a better sleeper she would not have gotten to this place. She would not have gotten to this dark place where she began to get angry at her mother, now, for pressuring her to be with a man she did not love.

But her mother brought her balloons all the time, and she brushed her hair one hundred strokes each night, and caressed sweet oil into her legs and arms, and told her always how very pretty she was. And she bought her beautiful clothes and ice cream cones and she let her yell and scream and cry. And she'd never yelled back. She'd never hit Mara, or ever yelled back.

And then things would be fine. She would be in her life, just in her life, until she went in to the bakery again and she would walk around and stare into magical cases and after picking just one he would hand her her treat wrapped in wax paper and then just as she was reaching out for it her mouth would start going—why did she always feel the need to go back?—and then her heart would start racing, and she'd complain complain complain…

Those lives

You can't see in the houses. They are all enclosed by tall walls. Though many have gates and are set back from the street so that sometimes you can get views of the gardens but not inside, not deep inside the houses. And you can't imagine the lives people live there. How do people get those houses? How do people get those lives? Though you know that they are happy, and that mothers live with fathers and the children they might bicker but they all love each other so much, and they eat food at a table which is set, and there is a woman who cleans up after them and keeps things tidy and washes underwear which she then folds and puts in a drawer all by themselves. A whole drawer full of clean and folded underwear, kept neat by the woman who gives their mother time to be their mother and take them to the park and sing to them and cook them such good food which they eat at a table which is set; and this mother she teaches them how to do things like wrap presents and tend to gardens and she kisses their father on the cheek when he comes home from work. At a real job. With an office. And, yes, you know that it's not perfect, that they fight sometimes and one time in their anger even threw things all around, but you know that there are lives there in those houses which you can only dream of, because you can never peer much past the gate and the front garden, never to the inside where the people live those lives.

They lived in an apartment building, in a tiny apartment and her mother worked and she went to school, sometimes, and at night, sometimes, her mother and she would go out.

Mexico City is a city of subways and busses and cars. It is large and there is money and there are trees and it is beautiful even when there is trash on the streets and bands of wild kids everywhere and the city is a lot of things though mostly you don't leave the neighborhood that houses the apartment where you live. But when you ride around in the cars of all those men you look out the window and the air sticks to your face while it all flies at you fast, and at this speed you see that Mexico City is a vast city of parks and fountains and people in groups and countless fairs and carnivals and beautiful restaurants and little food stands and Indian beggars and women and men in gorgeous clothing, and the children of these well dressed people always hold their parents' hands.

And in these rides through the city you sometimes see it from above like a French film as you sit in the back and you just look down, way way down from up there, at your mother where she sits in the front seat with that one man's arm tight around her shoulder sounding phony laughing too hard, and smoking cigarettes and then again laughing a fake laugh which goes on for way too long and then she holds her head back in guffaws so that you see her teeth, her ugly teeth; and you will not ever hold her hand, or anyone's hand, not ever, not ever again.

But there are the parks, your park, and alone you like to walk in it, and you sneak in to the movies, and when they're over you stop and smoke a cigarette. And when you walk on you look down mostly, and you don't talk to any other people, even though there are boys who walk around in groups and some are very handsome and there are girls and they stroll in groups too, and at school you meet a lot of them but those groups seem really pretty firm. But you don't care; you don't lift your eyes and you don't care because you don't need them, for your mother likes to go out, and there are lots of bars and a young girl can go out with her mother if Mother says she can.

And Mara doesn't like that old man.

Sometimes, late at night, from the front room Mara hears them in the bedroom. Her mother and a *boyfriend*, though she does not call them boyfriends, but Mara always does, because it doesn't seem so scary to her then. Boyfriend has friend in it, and though she knows that this is so lame, is the motion of a baby, still it makes her feel that then, with just that one word of amiable commitment, boyfriend, then really it can not be all that bad.

And as she lies there on her couch, hearing shrieks and grunts she thinks of that film where the man leaned back by the front door of the apartment building, leg perched up on the wall, cigarette in hand and the pretty girl with the short bob walked another man right past him then took this new man up into a room. And in the hallway this prettiest one of all the girls quietly greeted many others while they walked in and out of doors with no clothes on, being followed each by their own man all fully suited trailing right behind. My life to live. And the grunting and the shrieking don't seem so bad in French.

If her mother kept a job or if they stayed in one place, kept just one apartment then it would be easier on them both. But things get in the way of each other, because a new boyfriend often wants to do things and they almost always promise something and the combination of going out at night, day trips, and jobs do not mix well. And there is always the promise, with each one, of something better, so why even keep a job? And then apartments are lost and it is hard for her to hold on to friends who are so hard to make in the first place if you move around so much.

And there is this old man, now, and he loves her not her mother, and though his breath stinks—stale cigarettes and alcohol—her mother is constantly reminding that he has a lot more money than any of the past ones. Plus he travels back and forth from the US, is back and forth and back and forth so that there are always gifts, if she will just sit on his lap a little bit. Let him kiss there at her cheek and down her neck, a little bit.

But Mother hugs her and when she cries and throws a fit, only to let things out a bit, her mother loves her and caresses and smooths and pats with every kiss, some shiny earrings, or other pretty little gift in hand.

Nights like this

Let me tell you this. It *is* beautiful. The nights are beautiful. Especially when it is warm. And on an early evening when things are feeling calm they walk down past all those big houses where there is often music pouring out—Elvis, always Elvis, or the Beatles or sometimes, from the best house, the one that she imagines as a someday stand-in for her own house, Billie Holiday—to the park, together, and there are children, always children there running around parents, little tiny kids; and they, she and her mother, buy ice creams and they sit on the park bench and watch the children play. And there are lovers kissing in the shadows, and old couples who talk in whispers and stroll very very slow. There are nights like this too. When she feels inside a movie because it is warm and the air feels fine and she just wants to be in it in a dress and her flat shoes. Young people call out at each other. And girls smile in their tight skirts that they wear for the boys, all those handsome boys who call out.

If they have not yet had their dinner then on these nights they ask each other: What do you want to eat? and then she and her mother go down a list of good food, grilled meat tacos, or quesadillas or pork soup from the old woman's stand by the market, and then they go back and forth and argue as they try to choose. And they walk there, just the two of them and they sit at a table and they talk a little and she feels calm. For only a few minutes, though, because there is always something on the periphery, there is always something which catches her mother's attention and does not let her be. There is always this thing which Mara notices but does not see and this something keeps her mother from really looking or laughing or enjoying being here with her. There is always this in her mother that reminds her a little of a trapped animal, a little like it wants out, it wants out of the here and now, a little like there are better things, wilder more interesting exciting things, for her, out there, somewhere else.

And why does her mother not understand how delicious the breeze is against her skin? How delicious her food, how delicious her drink? Why isn't this enough? Why can't she just sit and smoke a cigarette and want to be here just with her? Why can't she just want this? Why can't she just be? But her eyes are always darting. Her sentences are short. And the only way that Mara can get a hug out of her is to cry and scream and say No No, No.

Routine being

Her favorite days now go like this: her mother gone, since the old man it is best if her mother is gone, no school of course, and lazy morning in apartment where she listens to her music and makes herself a quick egg and then slowly bathes and gets dressed so at noon she can walk down to the park where for an hour or so she watches the youngest children playing with their mothers, who never look her way. At two the brothers and the sisters, the uniformed and big kids come loudly rushing through, weighed down by leather backpacks which dance down spines and into hands. The hands go up then, and reaching out, arms catching at each other, another boy another girl and often with thumb counting fingers giving reasons for compliance or else pushing away and pulling back, boys and girls in joyful screaming, flying limbs, while the long haired quieter girls in knee length skirts and long wool socks whisper in each other's ears; and though she is much older, she wishes she were one of these.

But she is not, so turns away for she has somewhere else she has to be. A quick walk through the middle of the park past the raised and never once that she can remember officially used bandstand, though the children do use it for their hiding running chasing games; at two-thirty she sneaks past the ticket guy, whom she is sure always sees her though he pretends that he does not, and into the inside of the theater where she sits off to one corner in this way making sure that there's no chance that anyone will come and sit by her.

And then for two hours her eyes dart from the words at the bottom of the image to the actresses who move around so lovely on the screen, dart fast, so she does not miss a single breath. Afterwards, in the park it's long past lunch though not quite dinner so she doesn't have to rush home to see what Mother wants from her. And it is then that she begins to feel clearly very lonely, for she wants to tell someone what she has seen, what these movies mean to her, and of what this one has made her think. So she smokes her cigarette slow slow, and watches all the other people in her park, grown men and women mostly now, some lounging, others rushing through. And then again she feels so lonely and right across the street is that special little bakery.

Their slumber

There are times when you know things. You know what things are, what they mean. But on this night? You drive through this endless city fast, on this long confounding night. Near downtown, hitting every single red light the taxi stops sometimes for minutes at a time so you can really see the groups of women who stand on corners here; you slowly reach up, press your palm on the cold window; you can almost look into their eyes. Further on, traveling south, there are restaurants and nightclubs, four or five on every block, still open and with people so awake at this late hour pouring in and pouring out, laughing mostly, though sometimes serious and with arms around each other, talking so engaged, and you wonder who they are, how they know the ones they stand with, all so happy, all so caught up; all so fully in their lives. Your car moves, rushing past the tall buildings with five or ten mysteriously lit windows in each one and you try hard to see inside. And now on the small and discretely lit residential streets, you snake quiet, past the decent little houses, beautiful little gated houses, and everyone who lives in them peacefully asleep. The pretty parks in each *colonia*, dead now too.

You are dead.

And tonight you don't know what things mean. In this taxi as it speeds you home, you have no idea of what things are. You told him to go fast, your mother left behind, asleep now, like so many other people in the middle of this night, your mother asleep like a million other people in this city, in the middle of this night. As soon as she fell into her slumber, as soon as your mother and those two men all fell into their slumber—you there pretending to sleep too, your eyes shut, trying not to even breathe—as soon as they fell you snuck outside. Quiet now, you snuck, until you were outside. Then you ran, crying, and in the middle of your running you found a taxicab, and this man scared you too, it was a man driving that cab, *a man*, but he didn't even ask you why you cried. Where are you going? is all he asked. He must see hundreds of girls crying, you understand, thousands, millions every night. And you told him through your sobs: Home. 6050 Quito Avenue.

And now, safely off the street, safely in your ride, you think that it should never have occurred. Did that really happen? Your legs sore, the insides of your thighs.

Tomorrow, or maybe in a few days, you will go and see the baker. And you will tell him what just happened. You will tell him how you ran fast; they were sleeping. You didn't even cry until you were outside. But for now you are dead, right now you just need to remind yourself to breathe as you try to close your eyes. And maybe in a few days when you tell the baker, maybe in a few days when you pull it out of you and make him hear it, maybe then you can begin to feel you are alive.

And how last night

He says: "No, Mara, no. Don't tell me that."

"Yes," she says. "It's true. You have to listen to me now."

They are at a café. A little Chinese café, and when they walked in he said he knew how to bake those breads better than they do here.

As they sat he said, "The Chinese man should separate his butter." And when he said this Mara pulled out of her own thoughts and wondered how she ended up here, ended up in this place sitting right across from him, a man who talks about butter.

He closed his shop today, put up a sign, and they walked out, through the park and three blocks down, the first time they have walked out into the world together, and this fact of them outside, together, made them both so awkward that they didn't speak a word the whole way. For much of the walk on those bustling streets, though she did not know where they were going, she rushed nervous, three or four steps ahead of him. And this is where they ended up; he had to call her back for she had already scurried past, "This is it," he called out, pointing. "The best place around here for coffee and a treat," he added as she turned, confused, and floated slow right back to him.

And when they settle in and Mara begins to talk she instantly starts in with her mother, though today she had intended to put it off for a while, had decided *not* to tell him, to instead talk about the movie she's just sat through—sat through because of course she was just marking time, could not see a thing, her teeth biting so hard her lip had to beg them to let go, her nails scratching blankly back and forth at her legs and her arms and her neck from opening to final credits—had made a strong clear point to herself of postponing the telling, of maybe not telling, so why is it that she can not stick to this plan, that she is instead ranting about what she can not help but go on about, her mother, and why always in this tone, with him? and how last night they went out to a place where the men pay to dance with women and it was funny to them, to her and her mother, that men will actually pay just to dance with a woman, and the friend of her mother's who works there let Mara and her mother dance with men a bit. And they laughed. It was funny.

She hears her own voice like somebody else's rushing as it speaks; of course there is nothing she can do to slow it, impossible to stop. And she sees him look at her and there is something like pain in his eyes already so she keeps on talking fast; yes, it is the seeing it out in the world, there in his eyes, that propels her forward, makes her keep telling more, rushed, like this: And then her mother sat in a booth talking to this one man, the dim red light of the overhead lamp like a spotlight, and they talked as if they knew each other, smiling and with heads real close, though Mara had never seen his nearly drooling brutal face before. And after a bit they all stumbled out and into his car, not even a nice car, Mara and her mother and this man and then one more. And then they went someplace, not a hotel but a room and she didn't know how they got there but now they were inside and they were laughing and tonight she'd had a few drinks, just some rum and cokes. She had laughed with her mother at the place with the dancing but to tell the truth she had been nervous and so she'd had a few of the drinks the dancing men had bought. And then her mother and that man ended up on one bed and this other one he was drunk and stupid, could not say one thing; his hair sat like a black thatch on his dumb head and she did not say one thing too. There were two beds and it was not a hotel. And for just one moment they all sat silent, on the beds as if they were not that, as if they were couches or chairs instead of what they were. Then the air shifted and she felt her heart race and her head flipped toward the other bed, at her mother, and that man was on her mom now, and her mother was laughing, hard and loud, now; and through the noise she could see her mother's teeth, those crooked mother teeth. And then she blinked her eyes, her head spun and they closed for just one moment and now this man was on her too, and her mother and that man, the other one, they were laughing, together, rocking back and forth; and this was not a boyfriend, and he ended up with his head down in between her mother's legs. And then Mara closed her eyes and tried to think which one was this man and which one was the *other* one? And then the shes in her head got confused too, the she that was her mother and the one that was herself. And was *this* man between *her* legs; no that was her mother, and Mara closed her eyes a little bit.

And her head it is spinning, is this her head which is spinning? She has opened her eyes and is staring, staring up at the ceiling; she feels pain and hears grunts and she is staring.

She is dead.

Is it just that she has had too much to drink?

To his surprise

No," he says. He is looking away, his head slowly shaking back and forth, and even though his eyes are closed, she can tell that there are tears. There is a long pause and then he continues in a tight constricted voice, "Don't tell me any more. Don't, Mara." He is serious.

She looks down and sees his hands are fists.

But her heart is running in her chest when she says: "No. Yes. You have to listen; you have to listen to me. I know you think I'm special; I know you think you love me, but if I'm ever going to let you love me then you have to know some things about me and I'm going to tell you this."

"Shut up, please, Mara. Please. Just shut up," and he speaks even more softly this time, a mere whisper, his face still turned slightly to one side. Sad. Not the least little bit of disgust, she thinks, not a bit, not one bit of the disgust she carries deep inside. She hears only sadness in his voice. So much that she stops and hears herself what she's just said, and her heart is no longer racing because now that she has heard her telling with his ears she is crying too. And then her whole body is full of this crying, in a way that a heart could not ever race through. Her tears have forced her to slow, then stop, and in this pause she becomes afraid that she will disappear, be engulfed then disappear. So her brain starts running right away, for she has not yet told him how she got out, how she got away, and there are more stories—she wipes clumsily at her face with her hand like a paddle—other stories she must tell him, and now he will not ever hear. Because in the telling and not telling both, she understands now, disappearing seems too real.

And it is in this confused pause in her face right before she starts thinking that there is so much she wishes she could tell him, that he decides that he will take her. Take her far away from here. He has calmed himself now and has walked over to her side of the small booth, has taken hold of her little face-wiping hand and suddenly has his arms around her, is softly patting her head when he decides that he will say it: "I will take you far away from here. I will take care of you and to do that I must first take you. Take you out of here."

And to his surprise, Mara starts nodding, her eyes red and chest still heaving, nodding as if there is no other choice.

She is always so unclear. There is only the confusion. But last night. She'd felt terror; it still sat on the surface of her skin like a thick cream. Yet all she ever seemed able to do was to cry and scream at her mother, could never really say no to her mother. Maybe she should let him do what he would do. Take her far away from here. Maybe this would clear things up for her, and her head nodded more emphatically, maybe then she could be sharp and clear.

And now the Chinese man is walking over and he points and says, "What is the matter," and he tells the man it is okay, half triumphant at his conclusion, at the way he has decided, quickly found a firm solution: he will now take care of her.

But the Chinese man wants to know it just from her, he darts a finger toward her and says, "Are you okay?" and his voice sounds harsh, his pointing finger, though she reads that it is all fueled by concern. She nods, and then she bends her head down and when she does he sees the bruises on the back of her neck.

So then her boyfriend, he is now her boyfriend, takes her by the hand and they walk out and to the park where his heart runs while she smokes a cigarette.

And what about regret?

So he drives with determination. He has somewhere to go. And that somewhere is away from here. It is dawn now, the girl asleep there on the seat right next to him, her head propped up on the armrest, long hair falling into her face. Easy to reach out and touch her skin, lightly, soft; but he will not. She's so small, her sweet self curled into a ball with feet tucked under her on the seat; look at that little wrist. They are driving through the long harsh desert, softened now and made beautiful by the gorgeous pink glow of the rising sun. This soft light touches her little breathing mouth, lips slightly open, makes him want to kiss; but he will not. He is rushing her fast through this Mexican sun, does not know when he will see it again, and this hurts him in his chest, for he knows that sun in English is a vastly different thing. He knows he is moving away from this sun's romantically slow intrinsic motion toward something more mechanical. He glances away from that light, from the girl, and up into the rear view mirror, even though he knows there will be no other cars, nothing but what he is swiftly leaving from, and catches a glimpse of his own eyes. It is maybe odd that he never considers his own looks, is someone who focuses on what he does, but he knows he has nice eyes, bigger than average, dark-lashed. He knows too that she does not love them. He is sure he has a pleasant face, full lips and clear smooth skin, but he knows as well that he is awkward, is not easy in his body, stutters stupidly, is sickeningly shy, and of course this is what she sees. He is only at ease when he is making things, not like her, not like Mara, who shades everything she does in lovely, who floats instead of walking, and her hands, even when they're nervous, you just want to take in yours and kiss. Beautiful girl, sleeping angel with sweetly parted lips. He wants to do something for her. He wants to do all things for her. If she will only let him.

He thinks again of this new light they are moving toward and wishes things had not ended like they had with the American. Then he could go knock on his door. He'd arrive in the middle of the night, tired and wild eyed and like this he would explain. "Look," he would say, his voice running, "this girl needs our help." He'd be holding her up by the shoulders as evidence. And then together the two men could plan and feel convinced that they were rescuing a life. They would bend their heads in to each other and he would be happy, buoyed by this trusted older man's aid. If things hadn't ended in the way they ended, then he could go and ask for help. The old man would nod, say of course they could stay in his home. Then Mara and he would sleep together on the twin bed which had for two years been his; of course the American would not have touched his room. He had loved him, and so like a shrine it would sit, the bed right there, against the wall under the window he had once secretly crawled out of.

But, no, he knew he would probably have to let her have the bed to herself, so he'd sleep on the floor. And she could lie on her side and pet the old white cat, Fluff, who had already lived more than almost two decades, who was fat and healthy, so without a doubt would still be strutting about. Old Fluff was not a cat that could have died in so short a time, and so Mara would pet his white furry head, and lay around on the bed or the couch and be a girl, lazy, languorous and undirected, fingers lost in that white fur, until she figured out what she wanted to do with her life. It would probably take a few weeks.

In the evenings after work, he and the American could look in at her laying in the front room from the doorway to the kitchen and they could discuss her well-being together in hushed tones, serious though no longer anxious susurrations; and his plight, his and Mara's plight, could take on a larger weight through the concern, concentration and support of this kind older man. A larger weight in respect to the outside world, without seeming unmanageable, without feeling like it could swirl and churn and whirl and roll and get really out of hand, a mad and spinning bubble which held just the two of them. A soundless abrasive cyclone of confusion and mis-directed hostility spinning the lonely baffled pair. Because here, now, in this car with the beautiful sleeping Mara, with his mounting anger and worry, or was it worry then anger, here, now, he was afraid of the future for the first time in his life.

What would he do with this lovely, sleeping girl? He could ignore all the tears she'd cried last night. Pretend they had not poured out. At first he had asked her to stop; soon after stepping into the car his response to her loud sobs was a simple, "Don't cry, Mara." He'd waited a while, giving her a chance to pull herself together but when she didn't he had gone on: "Don't cry anymore; it's making me nervous and I have three days of driving on some pretty bad roads so neither one of us wants me to be nervous." But still she didn't stop, sad eyes leaking. After another hour or so of that incessant loud bawling he grew edgy and scared and so began again, entreating, "Please, Mara, you've done nothing but complain about your mother to me in the past; stop crying that you miss her; we have just begun. Besides where we're going there are parks, and there are movies too there, and there is a different kind of life. Remember the life you've left behind. Remember what your crazy mother did to you, what she got you into, how she used you." This is how he'd begged, making an effort to draw a contrast between what was, and what would come to be. With him.

But she had simply met his eyes and given him a look like he'd never seen and then looked away for good. Though she did quiet herself then, began crying silently, with no more heaves or gasps for air, her head resting on the window, private, and she hadn't turned to face him even when he'd tried to coax her out again. And of course it was worse, this, her private soundless weeping.

After about six hours he stopped and bought some home-made ham sandwiches and little baggies full of just-fried chips and sodas, all sold out of a basket by a black-shawled old woman next to where he'd stopped to get gas. He'd stepped back in the car and caressed at her soft shoulder—that skin made him want to cry—whispered her name; but she did not turn her head toward him. She'd refused, so he'd reached over and held the food under her face, though she had just rooted her head down and into the glass even further, so that it seemed she wanted to go through it, into another magical side, and when he'd accidentally touched her chin as he pulled his arm away he'd felt the tears mixed with snot that were running down her face. He wanted to yell. Fuck it! To take the food and throw it at the windshield and then have that glass crack and break spilling into a million little pieces which would come in and cut them both up. Then everything would come out on the surface, those cuts an actualizing of their inner turmoil, and they could wail openly together and then he could reach over and calm her down; put his arms around her and hold and hold. Kiss her on her mouth, the blood from their wounds mixing in their embrace. And then, after a good long time entwined, he would pull away and look into her eyes and say it was alright. That now they could begin.

But of course he did not yell, and did not throw a thing. He just placed the food down, in the large space of the bench seat between them, in the hopes that when he started driving again she would reach over and take his offering, one potato chip; but she had not.

That was when he'd stopped all the talking with which he'd begun the trip. All the attempts at drawing in, attempts at reasoning. It was all useless, and so he'd ceased.

If things had not ended in the way they'd ended with the American, that man would tell Mara about how change can be good. The American would stand there as an example of this as he nodded in a sage manner and tell her about his life before the train ride, about his orphan childhood on the streets of New York City before he was sent to live with his new family in the middle of that big land and about how when there is love a new life can be lived. He might gently take her hand as he said these things, look calm and deep into her eyes.

If he had not taken the money the American had hidden in the closet, if he had not stolen that cash then he could go back and ask for that man's help.

But how could he tell him that he regretted the taking, that he was sorry for having broken his trust? How could he offer to re-pay and then with the same breath ask for his help once again? How could he say that when he'd taken that money and then crawled out the window he hadn't known what he was doing, just wanted to change things for himself and for his father whom he was missing terribly that night, that he'd just wanted to return to the place where he felt comfortable, where he recognized the sun, and open a little bakery and then return one day and give the money back? How could he explain that when he'd gotten back to Mexico City his father had already died, in a drunken stupor he had heard, mortified by this final detail of that death, and that a month after finding this out he'd come upon that little shop that was for rent right near their old house and that it had felt like a new beginning to him, a new beginning in the shadow of their old life, a making right. And so he'd used that money on the shop and he'd slept on a cot in the back room and after a few months he'd gotten it all working; and every single day he thought about the American, the trust he'd shown, the way that he had picked him up off of the streets much as he had once been picked up himself; and then taught him how to bake, how to try at life.

He couldn't explain. He could not. He could not go there now, needing his help, dragging behind him a girl soggy in her own tears.

But as soon as he got them settled down, as soon as he got himself a job and found a little place for them to live, and got Mara into school or some such thing, then he would write to the American and tell him he was sorry and let him know that he was saving up to pay him back. He had almost gotten it all together but then this girl had needed saving, and this saving seemed more important than that other type of saving, though he would quickly start with that one once again. When things got settled down a bit.

And so he would have to watch Mara alone, from the doorway to the kitchen, from that little portico look out at her laying on the couch as she stared up at the tiny RCA tv that he'd come home with on the second day in their new place. Blank eyed, not smiling much or laughing, Mara, at the humor in a new language, at Dean Martin singing, strutting, singing right out toward her, as her belly grew and stretched and grew.

Indolence

It would not matter if he didn't love her. If he didn't love her he could tell her that her mother was a bitch, that he knew *she'd* done it for her mother's love—let herself be pulled around from man to man—but that her mother had no such excuse, had no reason, was plainly just depraved. She was a grown woman; she should have known better. Here he was, barely twenty, judging a grown woman and knowing he was right. If he didn't love her he could tell her she was sorry too. That she was a sorry bitch for wishing and waiting for that one man who would come and save her. Is that what she was doing? Is that what the far-fetched final purpose was? Because what man would take and save *her*? How bad off would he have to be to want *her*? She knew this too, and that is why she used Mara in the disgusting way she did. Your mother *used* you, Mara, he could have said. He could tell her the reality, the truth that he'd stitched up from all the different pieces of what she'd said. And he could ask her too: Have you really not put it all together? Come on Mara, he could say, you've known this all along. You know the truth too. Your mother is a horrible pathetic lazy woman who used you to try and get a better life for herself. And your father was a fucked up mean old drunk.

He caught himself, for what did he know about her father? Mara had never even mentioned the man.

If he didn't love her then he could tell her to find something to do. Nobody can just lie around and do nothing; nobody can become one with a couch. Do something. Pick up a book. If he didn't love her he could tell her to get up, sweep the floor once in a while, wash a dish, at the very least *watch* him while he cooked. While he made sauces and pots of rice, like he had for his father, like he had learned to do *for his father*, who had never said thank you. Who did nothing but gamble and drink. Please! he could yell at her, feed your cat!

In an attempt at giving her something, anything, at fulfilling his own months ago fantasy of her and Fluff at the American's, he'd come home with a little kitten; who in their right mind could resist a little grey kitten? But she wouldn't even feed him, barely lifted a hand at an attempted caress, though the cat would nuzzle right up to her, push up and into her big belly, trying to compete with what was inside for her warmth.

He had had to name the cat, because she would not even do that. Fluffy he had said, lamely, still using the American, he knew, scared at his aloneness without that older man. If he didn't love her, he could drive her back down to her mother. He should drive her back down to her mother and drop the sorry mess of a soggy pregnant daughter down and into her lap. See what you can lure with her now, he would work up the nerve to say. If he did not love her.

But, of course, he did. He did love her. He sees her as she walks into his shop on that first day. A wisp of a girl in a white dress. He feels his heart run in his chest, sees it leap out of his mouth as he stutters his first words to her when she comes up to pay, his tongue stumbling with the irregular beat of that racing blood pump. And this, this one vision would have been enough to hang many many dreams on, but then she comes back! The most beautiful girl he's ever seen and she comes back. And she picks out his pastries, eyes them with her slow pretty girl glow! And she talks to him! After a few visits she starts to confess her feelings to him. Her innermost thoughts. What joy! Who does he thank for this great joy? What has he done to deserve to hear this girl's distress? And when she lets him touch her, put his arms around her, at the Chinese man's only four months after they've first met, he almost melts, his hand on her shoulder. He wants to cry not in the same way he just had because of what she'd told him, the horrifying and sad details of her life, but because he has finally touched her skin. And when he sees the bruises on her neck he does not let himself imagine where they come from. He can not. Because he does love her. And so he sees them, notes them, his heart skips a beat before he chooses to ignore them, because they have a life to get to now. And all of this is past.

He does love her and in this moment of his touching her all of that is past.

A wish is not a life

But, of course, he realized as he put on his chef's hat, it was not past. That, probably, for them it would never be past. Like his father for him her mother had followed them here, all the way through one country and into another. She sat with them here in the air heavy and dark between them, taking up so much space that there was no room for them to speak to each other. Her mother and his father floated there in their apartment above and between and around them, making things happen, or not happen, controlling their actions or lack of action, sitting right there, hungry to take form in their two lives from so very far away; one life is never enough for a narcissist, he'd heard somebody once say, and until now he'd never known what they'd meant.

He stood here now, that automatic sun just coming up, in this empty but for him restaurant kitchen, in his chef's hat, having just dropped the dough onto the marble block and as it plopped out of the bowl he thought about how he knew, because he did love her, that he could not say anything to her about her mother ever again. Because when he had the last time he'd had to stop himself mid-sentence when he'd seen the same pain there in her eyes that he'd felt when people spoke of his father. Like a mirror, in her eyes, the mortification mixed with that inexplicable need to protect. My shielding him makes no sense but he's my father, he'd often wanted to say, my father, and that in itself is something, a love, that I can not explain. He'd seen her eyes articulating this to him about her mother the last time he'd allowed himself the liberty to say what he'd wanted to say. In the car on the drive to the States he hadn't thought of this, had mostly not seen her turned to the window face, so he'd proceeded, uncensored until her silence silenced him.

But then here, one day, when her wordless droopiness had made him insane—she did nothing but stare mutely at the tv, at the walls, at the air—he had said something, who even knew now what he'd allowed himself to say. Her look when she turned from the blank wall and met his eyes he did remember, though. He recognized it and he obeyed, stopped mid-sentence. And he knew that one of the things her look said was that though she could complain, this did not give him the liberty to say all he wanted to say. Then, of course—even though he had stopped, even though he'd run over to her and apologized for and retracted things he'd said, even though he reached out for her, took her little hands in his—she'd sat there limply, and slowly looked away; and then that thing that had started on the car ride up here, that silencing of herself became redoubled and now there was nothing, a heavy blankness, a weighty unarticulated space.

He had to admit, now, as he stood here alone in this kitchen pounding dough, that he *had* noticed it: the look she'd shot him in the car before she'd turned her face away was the same one, the look he'd now labeled a mirror. But at some level he'd chosen to ignore it so that he could attack her mother once again. He wanted to move his fist from the dough and punch himself in the face knowing, now, that it had been his sick need—to make himself look better by comparison, to make her want to be with him instead of her mother, to have her desire to share that skin— all his unquenchable need combined with an anger that she did not love him, did not appreciate him, did not want to be with him, that had compelled him to ignore that look and continue to berate.

And the expense of that thrill of attack was that the thing that had amazed him so much when it first happened, that opening up of her to him, that sharing, the confessing of a self, the openness of being for which he'd thanked the heavens, had stopped and he feared it would never ever happen between them again.

It was as if he'd violated something, and she would punish him for it in silence until the end of their days. She was so listless she barely breathed. What did she eat? He'd find a crumb there on the couch occasionally, testimony to a life, however slimmed down, while he was out. He would go to work early, as bakers must, open up the little restaurant where he made breads and cakes, and be home by three or four; and she would have moved, from a sleeping lump on the bed to a staring lump on the couch, and it had made him so angry and sad, her silence, that he'd stopped speaking too.

At first he had spoken, would narrate his days. Came home thrilled when he found the job, proud of his own cleverness and skill. It's one thing to have skill, but to be clever enough to show it off, that was something he had just discovered, something which the need to take care of somebody else had helped him to unearth. Like a traveling salesman he'd gone from restaurant to restaurant hawking tiny gorgeous cakes, little samples, and even though he knew he did not look the part of a baker it had only taken him two days, two days to find this pretty little place! But she had not responded when he'd excitedly shared his success. And then he had tried; had made many attempts; he'd come home with inane gossip about the two waitresses which he got from Ivan, the chef. He'd quote him, even imitate his gravelly voice: "Man, those two chicks drink so much they swim home every night," he'd repeated, laughing. And through Ivan he'd invent a future of mundane pleasures for them: "Oh, and he says that he and his wife went to Big Sur last week, says this is a beautiful place... maybe we can all go one day?" Like this he would concoct and talk and talk and it didn't come easy to him, this forced exuberance, yet he managed it though his attempts drew nothing because there she would lay not moving, wouldn't even nod or look his way. So, after a few months of this trying, he would mostly just look at her, quiet, no longer bringing life, other people's lives, into their place.

But then yesterday, six months after they'd arrived, he came in and saw her rocking herself back and forth, her arms around her belly, long hair streaming into her face, crying and rocking back and forth.

And he'd backed away from his observation spot there in the doorway and then banged around some in the kitchen so that she would know he was at home. When he walked back to the living room she was laying, like every other day, staring straight ahead. And then in the middle of the night he'd heard a noise outside and when he opened the door expecting maybe a skunk or a raccoon there she was instead, in the courtyard with her stomach showing clearly through sheer nightgown, barefoot and digging her feet into the dirt and when he went out to bring her in she turned with a face streaked in tears and features all distorted as she mumbled that she had to feel the ground, insisted that she had to root herself down, like a tree. "I'm a tree," she groaned when he approached her, "a tree." Her dirty feet.

And he'd had to pull her, weeping, had had to drag her in, though in those moments of tugging and pulling he'd felt it too, that she had turned into some kind of a strange being, a plant, yes, a tree, not moving or speaking, not living like a person should. "It's okay," he'd whispered over and over again, attempting to calm her as he walked her in, "It's okay."

He led her in through the door and washed her feet, put her into bed where, no longer crying, she stared straight.

"It's okay," he continued whispering to himself long after he'd left her there. "Okay."

And it was true her belly kept growing so that in those hours after he walked out of her room, shivering, he'd decided that some tending needed to occur.

Though now he could acknowledge he was frightened, he knew too that he'd decided; he must take tomorrow off; he'd made up his mind, his fist still pounding the dough; he would bake extra bread and cakes today so that he could take tomorrow off and drive her into town, to the doctor up the way.

Counterpoint

The next morning, still feeling scared yet soft and tender for the first time in a long while he got up and watched her sleep—her slow breathing, funny pot-belly rising and falling. He washed his face and looked into his own eyes, then shut them tight and kissed at the image of her little sleeping self that he drew up there before him. And then, with gentle whispered words, he got her up and bathed her skin. She did not respond to what he said but he kept whispering, narrating his actions, as he rubbed lotion on and into her arms, then ceased whispering as he thought of rubbing some onto that belly, before he stopped himself just shy of that intimate touch; he then dressed her in clothes he'd bought on his way home from work the day before, a sweater and skirt two sizes larger than when they'd arrived which he put on and zipped up for her, and some pretty pink leather shoes. The salesgirl had helped him pick it all out, sighing with delight when he told her who they were for, a sigh he wished he'd heard even once slip from Mara's lips, directed at him in that same salesgirl tender way, even if it were equally fake.

He brushed her hair, her beautiful long hair.

She stared straight while he did these things, eyes blank, then kept staring when, "To the doctor," he said. And she did not protest, her arms hanging there limply at her side, her skinny legs seeming heavy too now, her feet like roots with their plodding steps, as she let him lead her down and into the car.

Then his heart began to weigh in him; he felt it there in his chest; he'd only managed to buoy himself up for an hour in her presence and now he was falling again, and as he fell the brightness of the day began fuzzing grey around his head; and he forced himself to look away from Mara and out the window at what lay beyond their immediate oppressive space. Out the window, in a concentrated attempt to avoid the anger and worry he felt falling back down like a wicked mist upon him. He made himself focus on the world out there: the strange landscape, the outside, made odder still by his having so recently come from such a dense big city, the houses here spread so far apart. All these wide open fields with their wildflowers after this February and early March rain. The mountains mauve against the blue sky. In the distance and to the far right, Baldy, that one with the snow, he had been told. "Only a two hour drive and then boom, you're in it," Ivan had said. "You gotta go if you've never seen snow."

Ivan and his wife were always getting in the car and going places on his days off. "You should come some time," he had said, making it sound like an order. And he had not wanted to reply that his girl was not a wife, was not really his girl at all, that she was pregnant with another man's child; god, and how to describe her relation to that other man? That she was, in fact, herself a child who should be learning things at school. Isn't that what children do? And if these large and verifiable, easy to describe things he had not said, how to add that anyway, Mara never left the bed but for the couch, didn't speak, stared straight with dirty unwashed hair. How to add these things which were so painful to think even in shorthand, much more complex than physical actualities to put into words, ephemeral futility to describe. So, "Yes," he had answered instead. "Maybe one day."

The streets so wide and the light on this sunny day so incredibly bright. For a moment he did see beyond the misty grey that had descended like a veil inside their car, looked through and out the window to that bright California light. Hopeful again, now, he thought that if he were to hop on the Pasadena Freeway, which he had just passed, that historical little freeway with its curves and turns and tunnels and sycamore parks, he would end up at the American's in just five or six miles. Up in the hills in which the American lived, a place with the most American name one could imagine, Mount Washington, a place that in the middle of LA seemed really quite wild, with its canyons and countless hiking trails. Right up the street from the Indian Museum the American lived. He would go there, he decided. When the baby was born. No one can resist a baby. No one can stay angry in the midst of a little gurgling baby child.

But then he noticed that Mara stared out of the window too and this recalled their much longer, through two countries, six months ago drive. His stomach shuddered with the new definition he'd given yesterday to the memory of her last, piercingly hurt and angry look. He dropped his own head in shame as he pulled up right in front of the small craftsman house which held the office, reached gently toward her and in the moment his fingers touched her skin he decided that he would take her to Hollywood after this doctor's visit. He would try very very hard now. He would put himself aside and try very very hard to lift the misty grey from both their lives; he would show her some sights and then they would go to C.C. Brown's, which Ivan said had the best ice cream sundaes for many miles around. So good, Ivan had added, that they'd been the beginning of Judy Garland's tragic slow demise.

All the hearts

The doctor heard two. Of course this man did not see the heaviness of the girl's limbs, the disturbing vacant stare, could not know that her hair was not always so soft looking, clean smelling, could not image this strange young man's hands working at those greasy strands just two hours before. He did not see the pretty girl's months of self-imposed silence, the sleepless staring at darkness nights. This doctor man just listened to the facts and after checking her whole body, finger up inside, the almost solid truth of the through the stethoscope thump, thump thump thump thumping verified that there were two.

He spoke to the girl and when she did not answer, not having fully understood what he'd said, the doctor turned to the young man and repeated: "Get ready for some sleepless nights," and then he laughed. To the girl, not having noticed she didn't speak his language, that not much registered when he spoke, he said: "Eat more. And don't forget to exercise."

Then the doctor patted him on the back and said, "Yep, some sleepless nights. Good work, son. In approximately three months you'll be getting two for the price of one."

"Yes," he replied, eyes now glazed over: "I'm getting three for the price of one."

And with that he claimed to be the twins' father; with that he became the proud father of one, plus one.

More changes more

Her hair was clean. On their way back out to the car, Mara did not need his help. She could walk on her own, thank you. She liked her new shoes and her hair was very clean. She rubbed at her stomach and said it out loud: I like my new shoes. She saw him stumble at her words, knew that stumble was an outward show of the shock that reverberated inside. But no time to fully acknowledge that now, for the doctor had let her listen to their hearts. So this is why she was so big… there were two…. There were two little babies and she hadn't even really thought of it as one until she heard their hearts, and now she knew that there were two. And in the office she had seen some other girls, and a few of them seemed as young as her and some of those girls already had babies, were big bellied waiting for their second when already in their arms or even toddling about on wobbly little legs, they had a first; and she had smiled at the sight of those babies—her first smile in six months—their little baby wobbly walk, and for once she was not invisible, for some of those mothers had acknowledged and smiled back; and now to think that inside of her there was not one of those but two.

These babies, when they came in three months, would gurgle and coo and she would change their wee diapers and they would reach tiny arms up to her, these little baby two. If there were a girl and a boy she would name the girl Ramona, Mona she'd call her, and the boy would be Manuel, nothing for short, no need to call him anything but Manuel, and if there were two girls one would be named after her grandmother Francesca and then Mona, and if two boys Manuel and Oscar, but she hoped it would be one of each, though of course the four existed just as strongly and were as present as the virtual two, stories spun around them, personalities and adventures immediately created in detail, though over the coming three months she would add, making up more and more stories so that at least these four little individuals would be in place with many more particulars of their character set to really almost firm. The first-born girl would be bossy, that she already knew, though it would be minutes not years that she had on the other. The oldest boy, if a boy were first would be protective, at two or three he'd defend even his mother, her, though if the boy were younger he'd be angry a lot of the time at his older bossy sister. Who does she think she is—telling me what to do? he'd run protesting to his mother, her. She imagined them, the bossy older sister, the angry little boy, and the other two, for these were all the other options; what would they be, two girls, two boys? a lively virtual scene.

On the way to CC Brown's she told him all about it. If there were two this is the way it would be, but if there were four, and he looked at her, rather puzzled, There are two, he said, so that she'd had to explain, Yes, but if we move the numbers around, two girls, or two boys or a boy and a girl, and depending on who comes first, the girl or the boy the personalities will be so different, will surely be affected by this so there are girl boy, or boy girl, or girl girl, or boy boy; there are many more than just two. So let's just stop at four with my favorite combinations: girl boy, or girl girl. And he'd looked at her confused, but happy for her talking, she could see. She could see that he was happy for her voice. So he'd nodded when she'd repeated, Let's just stop at four.

And then in Hollywood, on *Hollywood Boulevard*! they'd walked some on the stars, she'd run screeching names she'd never even heard, and then she'd eaten all her sundae and then had some of his. And then she'd kept on talking about the boy and the girl or the girl and the girl or the boy and the boy; she couldn't wait three months to see!

There had been: The Only One

At night, she began to think of him. She hadn't let herself for a long time, or was it that she just hadn't, that nothing had come, that since soon after they'd left Mexico City everything had dried up so that there was nothing but a blank. A steely grey blank. But now things rushed at her quickly, especially at night. Though in the daytime too. It was true, she was thinking thinking thinking all the time. She was excited. She was anxious. She was eager. There were two. Her mind raced and leaped from thinking about those two babies in her belly to thinking of him, and all of the things he had shown her, the only one whom she had ever really loved.

They'd met him at a bar. It was a nice place; her mother had just gotten paid. And the bar had two levels so that from where they sat at the upper one they could look down and watch people drinking and talking down below. Her mother had seemed particularly bored, watching all the other people and not really answering when Mara talked. And of course, Mara tried harder, redoubled her efforts even though (or was it because) her mother was preoccupied. Then, although they were sitting up on top where you could really see, these two came from out of nowhere just as Mara was rushing through a story, forced laughter and enthusiasm, telling her mother about a boy and girl at school two years under her who were caught together in the bathroom and there was another boy who'd stood guard. Her mother just barely raised her eyebrows as she took a sip and then, her mother's mouth still on her straw, magically and out of nowhere these two suddenly descended. And the thing was, he was not particularly striking; the one talking to her mom—her mom who was now smiling, full of charm and animation—the one talking to her was better looking, taller too, but this one sat down slowly, leaned in gently, talked softly to her, and when she drank from her rum and coke he didn't try to rush her to a second; he just patiently sat back and continued to talk, measured and soft.

"Your hair is pretty," he said to her, and it didn't make her blush because he hadn't been overly general, overly enthusiastic in his praise; he'd picked out just one thing, and what's more he'd said it just kind of matter of fact.

And then—she could not remember how they decided it but they must have come to a decision—they all went for a ride together; the one with his arm around her mother drove the red Valiant, and she sat in the back seat with this one and did not even notice her mother, the way she so shrill laughed and tossed her head. Her mother disappeared, because now it was her and him back here alone and when he leaned over and pointed out monuments his arm brushed against her arm, her chin, rubbed along her chest; her heart raced as he pointed out the big golden angel which they were now passing up, kept running as he told her the story of that angel.

"It's a winged victory," he said, explained what that meant and then reminded her of the day it fell just nine years before. She had passed it hundreds of times, never even knew it had a story, only vaguely remembered the earthquake and then hearing about its fall.

Then they were in her apartment—and for the life of her she could not remember how they'd gotten there; she'd tried over and over to recall that lost hour or so because she wanted every minute for her hoard, but she could only get herself back to the four of them there in their apartment. She and the writer—she found out he was a history student who wanted to be a writer—

she and the writer were in the front room where she sometimes slept on the couch, and her mother had shut herself up with the friend in the bedroom.

"That's your mother?" she remembered him asking.

And she knew that there was pain in her face because now the friend and her mother, yes, it was her mother, were laughing and grunting and: "Yes," was all that she could say.

"Is it hard for you?" he had asked tenderly, and the question had never been asked; he understood and he sounded actually concerned.

"Yes," was all that she could say again.

And this is when he started talking to her about movies. He told her about this group of French guys, and how there was one theater, here next to the park in her neighborhood, that played all the movies they made. The only place in all of Mexico City where you could see these films, and it was just six blocks away. He told her he'd just seen that one that she then rushed out to see, the one with the girl in the short bob, with the boyfriend who was by the second or third scene not really a boyfriend at all so that he could have her go with all the other men. And he told her there was a novel and the movie was based on this French novel, and did she read? And when she said no he said that maybe she should try.

"I'll go see the movie," she'd replied.

"Okay," he'd laughed.

He talked softly until the sun was well up and then he'd said: "Okay," again, and kissed her on the cheek and said: "Good-bye sweet Mara of the beautiful hair."

She smelled and smelled at his pillow after he left, her head buried deep in his scent.

He'd lain there, reclining on pillows on the floor, all that night, and it was the most fun she had ever had and all they'd done was talk.

She went to see the movie the very next day, and this was something she didn't tell her mother because it was just hers and she'd never seen anything like it, the girl dancing with the pool cue. And you knew you were supposed to feel sorry for her, but somehow you just did not. And when she looked straight at you through the camera, God, you just did not.

And then Mara did not see him, but thought every day of him, his voice soft, large dark curls falling into his eyes. A writer, he said he was. She wondered what that could possibly mean.

And then he came again. A month! It had been almost a month when the friend, one night, began yelling up from by the parked Valiant where he stood with one leg still inside the ajar door up and out at her mom. So that her mother stuck her head out the ugly grey apartment building window and with her whole arm waved him up while Mara stood a few paces back. And her heart began to run wildly when the writer lurched out of his side of the car. She rushed back and sat down on the couch trying to look relaxed, bit at the inside of her cheek to keep herself from fainting as her mother opened the door, and as her mother and this new boyfriend exchanged kisses she caught her breath and barely looked up; the writer ambled over and then slugged at her arm "Hey" and "Hey" she said quietly back, releasing her breath though still not daring to look up.

And this time it was early so they went out for a walk. "Here, this is it," he pointed at the theater as they passed it by.

"I know," she answered. "I went to see the film you told me about," and she dropped her head way down.

He looked over at her, dropped his head down and into hers and she glanced at him sideways, still embarrassed and shy.

"Want an ice cream?" he asked, smiling up at her.

She nodded and then led him to the place that she always went to with her mother, "This is the best one," she said.

And then, ice cream in hand, they went and sat in the park. And here in the park they were perfectly quiet, watching little children, and old people, and young couples. And they licked at their ice creams and he didn't even try to hold her hand.

Then they walked back up to her place, and before they got to the door he stuck his arm in the parked car and pulled a bag out and then they went up to the third floor and then into the front room, and they heard the other two in their room, and this is when his talking began.

"I brought something," he said. He pulled the LP out from the bag and went over and crouched as he gently took it out of its sleeve and then lovingly placed it on the little portable stereo and then they listened to Billie Holiday. They lay side by side, heads real close on pillows on the floor and he translated lyrics as she lay still, almost holding her breath and staring up at the ceiling, listening to his soft voice dance circles around that voice which rose and fell and ran across bridges, and sank into lovely waterfalls.

And again he left when the sun was well up. And when the boyfriend came out hours later and gave her a look with raised eyebrows, it didn't matter who he was or what he thought.

One day the boyfriend came without him

He gave her *My Life to Live* and Billie Holiday and *The Four Hundred Blows*, where you were supposed to feel sorry and did, and there was a woman French guy and she made *Cleo from 5 to 7* and if only her mother were like the old woman in that film. And of course *Cleo* made her think a lot about what it would be like to be dying. To be beautiful and dying like that. A shortness of breath. And there was *A Woman is a Woman* and it was the same girl from *My Life to Live* only here she was even prettier if that seemed possible at all! And in this one she sang in the most glamorous blue outfit, matching hat and coat, that Mara had ever laid eyes on. And he brought a lot more music too but her favorites were the singing women, Billie Holiday of course, and Nina Simone, Ella Fitzgerald and one French woman, who was really South African but was Jewish and sang in English and when he put her on he said that nobody, no, nobody knew he had this; this was a very special recording only a few copies of which had ever been made. And all of these things she took and they were him but they were themselves too, and she wanted to make them a part of her. So that when she looked at things now she often compared them to things she had seen or songs she had heard with him. Her reflection in a shop window was her but now if she turned a little to the side and looked down, quickly up then down again, she was also a girl, a young woman, confused perhaps but nice to look at—sometimes even in a close up, a slow blinking of the eyes—the kind of girl who found it easy and pleasant to flirt at a café or a bar. And when she smoked a cigarette, she knew that if she blew the smoke out at just the right angle and curled her lip then she could be a man for just one second, Belmondo in *Breathless*, right at the beginning of the film, and this becoming a man for one moment would grant her the right to stare at young women, even their breasts, more directly than she would ever feel comfortable doing as a girl. And if she took and tied the sash of her raincoat quickly, firmly in a knot, she would look like she knew what she was doing. Like a woman who people said yes to, even when they wanted to say no, like Antoine's mother when she is walking out the door.

Everyone else their age dressed like Elvis, with rolled up t-shirt sleeves. But he wore skinny suits and thin thin ties not just at night when he went out, but all the time. And often he wore his dark glasses inside, and on him this did not look stupid and pretentious, but more like he was too busy to think about pulling them off just now for he had something to say, an important idea to get out.

He talked and talked so much to her, for that year, and most of it she didn't understand, too shy and embarrassed to ask him to explain, but the things she'd see in the movies he told her about, or the voices she heard in the music he brought, she applied to her life so that she knew that this was what they meant when they said that love can change your life.

One day the boyfriend came without him. And her heart raced as if she already knew. "Where is he," she asked trying to sound calm, trying to make her voice sound slightly offhand, "Where is he," she asked this one of raised eyebrows, this one of the stupid sneers, this one of the handsome face and practiced stance, with whom she rarely exchanged more than a hi. "Where is he?" she asked.

"Didn't he tell you?" he scoffed, brutal, leaning back on the counter and with big bare feet crossed at the ankle as he picked at his teeth. "Your *boyfriend* didn't tell you?" and here it looked like he was about to spit onto their floor. Or was it that he was going to laugh? "He went to France, ma petite, to study on a grant. Do you know what that is? Have you ever heard of a grant?"

And she looked down as she thought that she hadn't. She gulped hard as she thought that she hadn't heard of a grant. She didn't know what it was. She didn't know anything. She didn't know what anything was.

All the singing women

She meant nothing to him? How could he go just like that? And then when the two, her *mother* and that other one, had begun, she couldn't take it. She had run out of the door. How was it that he'd left? He didn't tell her? He'd been coming for a year, and though they'd never even held hands they'd lain together, on many many nights. She was going to count them. She would count them. And now she was in the park, her fingers rushing madly. How many, exactly, nights? It was true, he'd never come without the other one. That was true. But she'd assumed it was just something about the car. Though she had never even thought to ask him where he lived or if he had his own car. And they'd never really done anything together, just the two of them, besides going for walks and getting ice cream sometimes. And she knew that boyfriends and girlfriends were supposed to go out. And they had never even gone to one of their movies together; she always went alone. But he brought records. And they talked and talked all night. He did most of the talking, that was true too. But she didn't know anything. How could she have done more of the talking when she didn't know what anything was? And, besides, there was this too: a couple of times he had told her she was pretty and he'd run his hands through her hair once or twice.

Had there been a look the last time he was there? He and the boyfriend had let a month go by, again, like the first time. And she was upset. Told him about herself and her mother at a bar. How many people had come up to talk to them. And there had been something like disgust in his eyes. Had there been something like disgust in his eyes?

She'd been upset and wanted him to know that other people felt her pretty, worthy of a chat. Why don't you come more often? Where have you been all this time? If only she could have yelled these things, but no, instead she'd talked about herself and her mother, talked about herself and her mother when she just wanted to ask him what this was. When she had just wanted to tell him that she thought she was in love. And instead it had been all the men at some bar. But when she saw the look, she regretted it. Was there a look? Had there been a look of disgust? There couldn't have been; he had always been so kind. Regardless, she had changed the subject, asked him what music he'd brought. She'd really liked the last one; she lied for it had just been trumpets and horns, and a million times she'd said she liked the voices, the women singing more, though of course she had not added that his voice when he translated, his voice lacing gently around their voices was the part she liked the most.

"Did you? Like the last one?" he'd asked. "Have you started to like Miles?" So that he must have known that she had lied. Had he asked because he knew that she had lied?

"Yes. Though I like the singing more," she'd tried to make it up, had tried to sound nonchalant. "Of course, you know I like the singing women more."

But no, that could not have been it. There had not been a strange look because then they'd gone on to have a good night. He had brought a bunch of singing women. All doing one song, Sathima Benjamin, the Jewish French woman who sang in English and was really from Africa and whom she was not supposed to tell he had. And Billie Holiday. And then one other she'd forgotten. She had memorized almost all the names, because for the first time in her life she was ashamed that she knew nothing. She wanted to know at least the things he'd shown her, she wanted to be able to hold on to these things, to know at least that these things were something that she had.

It had been a good night. There had not been a look because he'd put them on, one after the other, all singing the same lyrics, and though it was the same words over and over again, three times, he translated each and every time: *Darn that dream I dream each night/ You say you love me and you hold me tight/ But when I awake, you're out of sight/ Oh, darn that dream/ Darn your lips and darn your eyes/ They lift me high above the moonlit skies/ Then I tumble out of paradise/ Oh, darn that dream/ Darn that one-track mind of mine/ I can't understand that you don't care/ Just to change the mood I'm in/ I'd welcome a nice old nightmare/ Darn that dream and bless it too/ Without that dream, I never would have you/ But it haunts me and it won't come true/ Oh, darn that dream* three times, different women had through him sang, or he through them.

It must have meant something and it had not been a bad night.

For a year Manuel had been coming to see her. Two weeks before she turned fifteen they'd met him at the bar and then just a week before sixteen had been his last time. And then a month later her mother and she met the old man, and her heart was already broken, her heart was already broken when her mother started trying to shove on her that leering old man.

And though they never had even held hands, she made herself believe that the babies in her tummy, that these two inside her belly, were his. Their father was a writer. Their father was a writer who had moved to France on a grant.

In the garden

At night, her eyes searching the ceiling for clues, Mara recalled more and more images from her past. Her head sifted and pulled together and tried to make sense of separate, like scenes from different movies, pieces of her past; yes, it was less like recalling and more like trying to make sense of scenes that came rushing at her which she barely recognized as her own life. Her belly big, and not letting her sleep, her belly big and promising a future, a tomorrow of little children, after for so long, for six months, not being able to think of anything, not being able to imagine a some day, or more confusingly, to even reach back into a childhood she had maybe never had. Had she ever been a child? When she saw children she knew that she had never been like that. She had never run, and thrown her arms in the air, and flipped around on the grass. And now she was moving back and forth from these two options, the then and the to be, without ever really stopping at the present, at this place in California, what was this place in California? where she lay staring at the ceiling far into the night.

Yet she'd had places she had loved. She'd had places that were not a question to her, that were firmly in her mind. There had been a big garden at her grandmother's house, for one. She hadn't been there for over six years, since her grandmother had died, but there had been a big garden at her grandmother's house. And there was a girl who lived with her grandmother and was the maid's daughter and this girl's name was Patricia and they called her Bibi and Bibi and she ran around together in these periods when they spent long stretches there at her grandmother's house, sometimes for months and months at a time. Until her mother and her grandmother could not stand each other any longer. Because though Mara did not understand it their general distaste was always there though it hid in wait beneath the surface for a while when they arrived, and emerged slow, at first showing its head only in a quick though wounding word or two flung out at each other; though its breadth showed in the coming days in the volcanic angry bursts which within a few more weeks grew into intense short arguments from which they both retreated hurt. And then it came out brazen, expanded itself hungrily into longer and more involved disagreements so that within a month or two the screaming turned to tears for a whole day, then for many consecutive days, before neither one of the women could stand to feed it any longer and mother packed them up and they'd go off, without warning and so no good-byes. Confused little Mara, her arm held stiffly up, trying to balance on awkward shuffling feet, as by her mother's engulfing hand she was once again being pulled away from her Francesca.

But, when her mother lost another job, or when a new boyfriend had gone off, or when they were kicked out of an apartment and a new one not yet found, they always came back. And in these times of being here her Mother disappeared for days on end so that it was Bibi and Mara in the garden.

Bibi always immediately welcomed her back, a grabbing of hands—not even a pause—and then she and Mara would spend their time making things up. So that Bibi, seven, and Mara, eight, one day made a game of feeding little black and yellow grasshoppers to some spiders that lived in the recessed cracks in the wall between this house and the next. In these dark places big furry-legged spiders had made their secret homes. And Bibi had on this day taken the little grasshopper Mara had found and caught—she'd snuck up on the insect focused and intent as it sat on leafy geranium, careful and with cupped hands and then Bibi had abruptly snatched it from her and carried it over to the wall and purposefully fed it to the spider who sat waiting anxious but discreet deep in its dark cave. No, Bibi, she had wanted to say, but hadn't. No, she had wanted to say, but had not.

And then they did this all that day. Sometimes, after Bibi had thrown it in, the grasshopper was able to pull free of the web and other times the spider would crawl slowly towards it as it struggled to get free, Spider finally quickly reaching out with its thick and bristly arms before clumsily pulling its feed back into the cavernous recesses of the dark crack. And then the girls would groan and Bibi would squeal with delight: "Did you see its hairy legs?"

Mara was both disgusted and thrilled by this game. She never told Bibi to stop it. And though each time she wanted to tell her not to do it again, she continued trapping the grasshoppers and then, each time, shared in the shriek of delight.

The sun was coming down now, and her mother who had been gone for nearly a week walked in the gate silent so that the girls did not see her until the spider's black legs reached out for the still squirming insect. "I used to do that," Mother said. And it was only then that the girls turned, suddenly, as if caught, and saw her there, in the falling shadow of that late afternoon standing in her black dress and high heels right above their heads. "I used to love doing that," her Mother said, her eyes blank.

Mara had kept staring as her mother turned and walked into the house, and then for a long time after she heard her mother's voice in her own head, the blank low-toned pleasure in her: I used to love doing that.

There was a day, there in that garden, on which it rained frogs. She could not remember seeing them fall from the sky in that way, one inside each drop of water, but that's how her grandmother Francesca told her it had happened and Mara only half believed it even then. However it had happened she and Bibi ran for glasses and they filled each with the tiny little frogs which now littered the garden and then ran into the house for water from the faucet which they poured over them to half full. But when the tiny frogs, now lined in long rows of glasses in the front room, began jumping out they had to rush them back outside from inside of the house, two glasses at a time. For Teresa, Bibi's mother, had sternly told her and Bibi that her grandmother would not like the kitchen and the front room full of all these little jumping black spots, so they'd run yelling orders at each other, water sloshing, before she came out from her nap. And then later, after Bibi had gone to her room with Teresa, Mara asked her grandmother if it had really rained frogs, and the old woman answered that yes, one inside each drop. And then that night as they were getting ready for bed Mara told her mother this.

"No, it didn't rain frogs," her mother tersely quieted her excitement, and then continued, exasperated, confronting her daughter's confused and worried look with: "Come on, Mara. I'm too tired for this stupid game. Your grandmother is making fun of you. She's like that. She makes things up all the time."

No, she doesn't, she had wanted to say. My grandmother does not make fun of me. And she does not lie. But instead she had just stared as her mother looked at her own reflection in the mirror while continuing to repeatedly pull the big brush through her short black hair under the bulb of the electric light.

One day, Mara went to the market with her grandmother. On the way home Francesca gave her one of the apples she had bought and Mara ate it, quiet, as they walked. It was on her third or fourth bite that she noticed a worm in the apple, down near the core; Mara shuddered and showed it to her grandmother who inspected it, and then threw it on the street. "Do you want another?" the old woman asked, matter of fact. She shivered as she answered that she did not. And when she turned back to look at the apple that only an instant before had been thrown down she saw an Indian girl, bigger than herself, but poor, a beggar maybe, wrapped in a ragged black shawl. She had come out of nowhere and Mara watched as this ghost girl looked deep into her eyes while taking her first bite.

They were the same person, she and that girl. There was something in that look, in the directness of her gaze. She pulled her eyes away but could not stop thinking of that girl who was and was not her, eating an apple with a worm in its center, there before her eyes.

When she got home Mara told her mother this, and her mother did not even raise her face from the black skirt that she was wiping with damp cloth.

She slept with her mother, in the same bed, unless there was a boyfriend around. And here at her grandmother's house there was a picture of an angel on the wall behind that bed; it was a picture she'd seen many times, in other places, and her grandmother had told her that it was a guardian angel and Mara was confused by this. In the picture the angel is huge with long golden hair and big white wings and her large hand sits under the broken slats of a high bridge a boy and a girl are crossing. Her hand saves them, keeps them from falling through those broken-off slats. Her large hand guards their safe crossing. "And you know when you look at it," her grandmother had said, "that this is only one time, one example of her constant careful guard. There she is, right next to them, always, even though they do not see her."

Mara sat on the bed and looked at this picture, now, more closely; she was understanding for the first time: it was a *guardian angel*; you did not have to see her to know that she was there, and she stood up on that bed to get a better look. Because in a picture you could see her, the angel's beautiful long hair, a boy and a girl smaller than her, and her mother looked over from in front of the mirror, through the mirror, so that it was the back of her head and her face both which Mara turned and saw when she began to speak.

"She pulls her hand back sometimes," her mother said.

"What?" Mara asked, confused.

"Just to see what will happen. She pulls her hand back. Otherwise how would accidents ever happen? How would people ever die?"

Mara stared through the mirror, deep into her mother's eyes, not understanding and terrified, unable to talk. And then that night in bed, her own eyes looking past the picture and at the ceiling, no longer able to focus her gaze on that scene she wondered if she was a girl from whom an angel would pull back her hand.

She slept with her mother, in the same bed, unless there was a boyfriend around, and on most nights Mara would tell her mother things, try to get her to talk with her before they said goodnight. Her mother was always having to hush her. Mara would stay awake, her mind still racing, as her mother's deep breathing turned into tiny consecutive snores running deep into the night.

And now her mother was gone. It was true that Mara had left her. But in some way she had to admit to herself, now, that there had been no leaving her mother, because her mother had always already been gone.

Bi... Bi...

Bibi often sat in Francesca's patio room while Mara trimmed flowers or planted or pulled weeds with her grandmother. This was a room Mara didn't like. She did not like going into this room and Bibi had made fun of her, telling her she knew she was a chicken, a coward, fraidy-cat.

She was not really afraid, but it was so gloomy in there; it was a long narrow room with no windows, who could like that? and then just that one door and a little bathroom tucked into the back. And there were these dark colored paintings stored in there, painted by her now dead great grandfather Andres, Francesca's father. They were of a brother and sister he had left behind in Spain; their creepy green eyes followed you wherever you went. They had both died of fevers the year after he left. She had had fevers, and she wondered how hot you had to get before a fever could make you dead.

Sometimes Mara would look in on Bibi from the doorway, sneaky so Bibi would not see. And what Mara could see was that Bibi mostly just sat there looking at those paintings, direct and unafraid, staring back into their eyes.

Just before her grandmother died she'd asked to be moved into this room; she wanted to be near the garden, she said, as close to in it as she could be. So her grandmother lay in this long room like a coffin all day and all night, like she was already dead, and though this was scary to Mara it was not so to Bibi. Every day Bibi would open the heavy door, pushing hard with both of her hands and then she'd ask Francesca if she was okay and the old woman always nodded yes. Then, her job done, Bibi would step back out into the garden where Mara would be waiting, finishing the piece of bread and cup of warm milk which Teresa had given her, and then they would begin their games.

"Grandma Francesca likes the light that comes in from the patio," Bibi once announced.

"I know," Mara had answered, confused, because she had never heard Bibi call her grandmother Grandma before, though she knew people did this all the time, that she herself had lots of women she called aunts who were not her aunts, for instance.

"That little bit gets bigger as the day goes on, creeping further and further in before finally fading out," Bibi went on.

Mara could *see* that her grandmother liked it because the old woman nodded at Bibi every morning when she went in, like she was glad to see her. Glad to get some fresh air. Glad to get some light.

They spent three full months there, at her grandmother's house, that last time, before her grandmother died. And through watching Bibi Mara got braver toward the end of that final stay—before her uncle moved in and she and her mother were not allowed back—so that she began going into the patio room too. And pretty soon the only thing that Mara came to mind in that room was the smell. Toward the end of that final stay she could sit in there for hours and watch her suddenly ancient grandmother open and shut her eyes. She could watch as her grandmother shut her eyes slowly, the paper-thin lids all covered in veins, and then kept them like that for whole minutes at a time, breathing short shallow breaths like a tired out dog before opening them, slowly again. In the year since they'd lived with her last her grandmother's skin had turned into paper. Sometimes she would take her grandmother's hand. Francesca would slowly reach out to her and Mara would take it in one of her own hands and then rub at it with her fingers, feeling the dry and fragile skin.

One day as Mara was walking toward the patio room she heard first, and then from the shadowy doorway saw Bibi talking at grandmother Francesca, and it was a different tone of voice, a different force, a way of talking Mara was not familiar with: "What's my name?" Bibi had asked in that serious tone, "Do you know my name?" Mara saw that her grandmother just stared. "What's my name?" and Bibi inched down, by the old woman's face, "Who am I?" she insisted, "What's my name?" She was saying it harshly now and Mara grew frightened of her friend, "What is it? Do you know who I am? Say it." And Mara saw the old woman's lips move slightly and then she heard a very low and repetitive: "Pa… Pa…"

And then a couple of weeks later her grandmother was dead, and she and her mother never went back. As she understood it, her uncle had given her mother some money, which was soon spent, and then he moved into that house; and Mara thought that maybe one day she would find the house and go and see them, because although she barely knew her uncle and although her mother had made a point of telling Mara that Bibi and Teresa and her uncle were all trouble, that she didn't know how his wife, her aunt, put up with it, she had also mentioned that Bibi and Teresa would probably always be there, that unlike she and her mother (and in spite of her dimwit aunt) those dirty interlopers would never ever be made to leave in the humiliating and awful way that they had.

Her grandmother was the one person who had felt safe. But now she was dead. And Mara had been cast out. And if in twenty, thirty years, she did manage to find her way back to that house, it would be Bibi's unflinching and calculating eye peering through that peephole, deciding whether it was really such a good idea to turn the knob and let her childhood friend inside.

Mine

She looked happy, now, and he wanted to touch her. That she knew. Though in the places he could not see, on the inside, there was much more: a constant nervousness and worry and unease; a strong sensation which felt electric and racing, unmeasured, and which sat just under the surface of her skin at all times so that she knew it well but could not put straight language to. Her mind rushed constantly too, in these violently vivid short scenes of her life, intense and separate and disconnected, like not her life at all. Where was she in all of that? a not Mara, mere shadow, a ghost, there and not there at the same time. Her sense of her self so confusing. What was this blurry *she* which inhabited *her* life?

Yet from the outside, to him, she was sure she looked real and fully there, content even, as the numbness fell away and now she talked and listened to the radio or watched tv in English or sometimes even sang. She was learning English. She'd been soaking it up for seven long months, and now it would fall out in short sentences, or in longer stitched together complex phrases through the songs. And though very little of what she did really meant anything at all, she could do so much at once now. And this, all of this, she understood, must have made him want to touch her even more, her new aliveness, her newfound if spotty and undirected interactions. Fluffy had grown fat, because this was another thing she did these days; she constantly fed the cat, huge piles of food that the previously neglected animal must have read as love, so that it did not know when to stop swallowing it all up. She'd stand there and stare as he ate, in this, at least, self-satisfied.

And she walked and walked, tentative at first, just around the block, for these streets were not familiar, were not her streets at all; even so within days she'd made it down two, three, more than five. And though she understood that to him this also simply looked like action, like she was finally doing instead of just staring into greyness, he could not have known what these long walks meant to her insides, all those inside private parts. Or to whom they led her. Or that she walked, as well, to get away from him.

Sometimes, on a very sunny and clear day she was able to look outside too, to really tell there was a world out there and that this peculiar almost always bright sun world she now inhabited in this far off land was full of strange low houses, wood mostly, far apart, all with immensely long front lawns. And they looked like the houses in picture books, windows and doors like stern angry faces looking out and making judgment on her. On second thought they were not so far apart, these disapproving wooden houses, and because of the way they were all lined up straight like eager soldiers, and all of that green grass, just looked further apart than in Mexico City where houses were made of stone and cement and were positioned quite variously on their lots. Here it was long green in front and then also on both sides of this army of serious faces; though if you were feeling particularly brave you could look right back at them, confront those windows like eyes, because there were no tall walls stopping you from peering inside. There were no enclosed gardens with tall walls that led right up to sidewalks, closing off the gaze, like you saw everywhere in Mexico City with its private insides.

And in many areas between these flat one-story houses there were big open fields, and all that openness of space was strange too, though it, at least, was beautiful and she had her favorite of these fields, had reason to crawl into them and shut her eyes, and now after the rains the untended grasses in them grew so high and wild-flowers opened up and out toward the sky in such reds and oranges and purples, soft pinks and yellows that could enclose her, embrace amidst intensity of shades.

And there was this: She was furious at her mother.

She saw him there, then, before her as she walked, the big man that dwelt deep in one of her fields. He stood tall amid that green and red and purple, coaxed her over with a sinewy finger. But she didn't want to see him now. Not today. "I don't want to talk to you today!" she screamed, angry at his intrusion.

"Don't shout, Mara," he said low and calm. And his steady tone compelled her to walk to him, his thick black hair, strange crooked smiling mouth, a line instead of lips. "She didn't mean to do it, you know," he added softly. He raised his hand up to her face and reached to touch, "She had no idea how you felt."

"Yes, yes she did!" she screamed again, backing away from his searching fingers. "She pretended she didn't know it, but she did." And here her voice grew quiet, "The way she always dragged me with her. In and out of groups. Like two lost fish. All those hovering men. At home I would cry and tell her no. Throw myself down and scream. I didn't want to go next time, didn't want to have to be there."

She was deep in it, now, the field. She was so tired. She lay down. And he sat himself gently next to her, his big protruding fish eyes, brown; he took his heavy hand and clumsily caressed her head, though it did not soothe. "But you liked it too," there was a tinge of mocking sharpness to his tone now. "You dressed up, loved all the pretty dresses, brushed and brushed your hair and put on make-up. Made yourself lovely, enticing."

"No, I didn't…"

"Yes, Mara, you did. I was there. And your mother didn't know any better. She wanted a better life for you, pretty things. She loved you Mara, and you just up and left."

"No," she insisted, shaking her head. It was not so unclear. Her mother had done this to her. And, her mother had pushed her on the old man. Her laughing mouth, that strong womanly stench. Overpowering all her senses. Loud in public but low, controlled and convincing when at home, and wicked too, dangling presents like carrots. And she a dope. A stupid Mara. Stupid stupid fish. A great big swallowed up she.

She looked up at him, pushed away at his annoying caressing hand, and sprang up. "He looked like you," she said, her heart suddenly running, "his ugly black hair like a thatch, so drunk his skin looked green, so drunk he almost fell asleep—if only he had fallen, dead weight there on top of me, instead of spreading me open and pushing his pants down, not even off, so drunk and eager at the same time, his sick self pressing up and into. My head spinning, heart leaping; and then I think I died."

"You didn't die, Mara. Here you are."

She heard her own voice and looked over at him; but he was gone. "It *was* death the stopping breathing, pulling back of the hand and then the stillness. The disappearing."

Mara placed her fingers on her mouth as if in that way she would be able to stop the words which she managed to push deep back into her head now, but that lame hand on mouth had no power, for no matter what she did, how hard she pressed down, her head kept racing crazy.

She looked around for him again, but he was really gone.

Since she'd told the baker at the Chinese man's the day after it happened she had not even allowed herself to think it and now she had said it, hushed but she had said it. She held her lips tight, teeth biting, rose up and walked out of that field.

The next day she walked fast, her head down. Nevertheless, out of the corner of her eye she saw that little figure running quickly, a slight silhouette speeding into grass. It was difficult, she was so weighted down, but she ran too, a hundred steps into the field before she had to stop.

"You're so slow," said little Francesca, disdain in her voice. Mara walked toward her, exhausted, lay down on the grass, "How do you ever expect to catch me like that?" the girl went on.

"You're hair's a mess," Mara said softly, reaching her hand up toward the child.

"So?"

"Come, let me touch you. Look at your lovely face," Mara had tears in her eyes.

"Stop it. Please."

At that the other three approached.

"What are you doing? Lying in the grass like that?" Patricia asked, and then she went and lay by her.

"If this were snow we could make angels," said Manuel as he dropped himself down with a thud and then started to whip his arms and legs about wildly.

Mona came and stood over him and smiled, "You can't make angels out of grass," she said matter of factly.

"You should come home with me today and let me bathe you, let me wash your hair," Mara whispered, moving her eyes from child to child. "Then I can take you to the park, and like all the other children you can run and play with sand, and I will buy a balloon for each of you, a simple present, not a bribe for some scary pact…" she must stop. The children should not hear that.

"Let's go home," she said reaching toward them now, "and I will give you kisses and we can sit and look into each other's eyes and talk and sing and hold each other's hands. I can keep you warm."

"You can't," said Francesca. "Look at you; you can't even get up. You can't take care of yourself, that fat cat, so what makes you think you can do anything for us?"

"She's right, you know," said Patricia. "It's sad, but you're sick. And your mother was sick. And regardless of what you do, we are going to be sick too."

Manuel's arms and legs were still going, only now the motions looked like a series of spasms, a seizure, as if he'd lost motor control. Undisturbed by this jerking, Mona got down on her knees and tickled under his arms, his neck, little belly, and his laughter took over the other more unsettling physical motion so strong and deep that soon Mona was laughing too and then they both collapsed.

"That's not true," Mara's face was very serious; she looked intent into each set of eyes, worked hard to sit herself up, "I *will* take care of you. I'll send you to school where you'll make friends and together we'll learn things and I'll show you movies and play you songs which we'll all sing together and every night we'll dance."

"Sorry, Mama," said Patricia.

"Call her Mara," Franc insisted. "Anyway, sorry. Patricia's right. None of that is going to happen. Impossible. Now, good-bye..." and the children all ran off.

Mara didn't have the energy to follow. She just stayed in her field for a long time, laid her head back down, and tried to control her speeding breath. But before she rose she decided she did not believe them. They were wrong. She would be that kind of Mama; she would be able to do all of that.

She made her way back home and there he was and like every other day she talked to him too, the baker, made her voice normal and conversed about nothing mostly, talked in a different way than she talked on her walks, of course, because with them it felt urgent; it flowed out from deep inside. With the baker it was conscious, an effort. With him it was all talk about the long lawns, or Fluffy the fat cat, or about kicking from inside which she felt now as an answer to her hand pressing down upon them through her stomach, or how in April it was already so very very hot. It was always talk about physical things, external things, which did not really matter, not the big stuff like the past with her mother or the future with the twins, because, to be truthful, she did not see him in either of these times.

Yet she knew that to him the kind of talking which she offered was enough for he would reach for her in the kitchen thinking she was happy, that her racing voice meant that she was happy, and a few times he tried to put his arms around her but she would always pull back, pretending the recoil was not intentional, she was just reaching for her glass. And with this type of excuse she would always draw herself back.

She knew how it looked to him, all her talking and sometimes smiling, but there was no possibility for touching for he in the past had tried to control her and she had not too long ago realized that the thing that had happened to her here was that once again she had not been allowed to have something that was just hers, something that she could hold magically yet firmly like an object and say: it's mine. And for all this time with him now she'd had nothing at all because he had taken it when he had sharply silenced her in the car. She *had* shared with him; she had told him many many things before the car. But he had become, in his shaming remarks, in those mean comments, had become just like her mother, controlling her, in a different way, maybe—he had done it with his judgments for she knew that he did judge her, how could he so harshly judge her mother without it somehow flowing through and down to her? So that when he reached arms toward her, now, she drew away from him, wanting to keep something, something of the newfound freedom of her open anger at her mother, of her future with the babies now inside her, of the all hers she had found in the act of being pregnant. Mine, she wanted to yell at him, though she didn't. Mine.

One day she saw her mother, she ran toward her first, but then stopped, backed up a few steps and from here began to speak: "Why didn't you ever talk to me, direct. Look into my eyes. Or kiss me just from pure love. On the cheek. Near my ear. Or rub my head like I've seen other mothers do. I know it happens. Or whisper to me about love you felt for just me, rather than only when trying to talk me into sitting next to someone who might help you get something you might want?"

Her mother just stood there silent. No response. Mara stared to see if she would even blink. And then tired, so overwhelmingly tired, she sat with some effort, adjusting her belly carefully with one hand. On the curb in front of that empty lot her words came together slowly now as she began to cry. "Why didn't you ever just hold my hand, sit in silence with me, just be there, my mother next to me, my mother, instead of making me feel like I had to entertain you just to hold your interest for more than one minute at a time?

"Why couldn't you just tell me stories, make-believe stories, just for the wonder that they gave me, instead of needing to break everything down. Break it down. Break me down. So that I had nothing, nothing that was magically mine?"

Mara. On the curb. In her head. No longer surrounded by far apart houses, by spread to the sky color of flowers, her mother there, before her, no outside world any longer. Just her and her mama. She crawled to the middle of that field and lay down, stared up at the sky and stopped crying. Wished herself a plant; shut her eyes and tried to sleep then; she was sadly not a tree. Shut her eyes and tried; but she could not. And then furious again, and disconsolate, her voice came out loudly, so that she heard it, her now shrill voice coming out: "How could you!"

She walked home fast that day. And when she got there, there he was. His mere presence made her mad now. The mean and angry silence with which he had answered her desolation, her sorrow at leaving her mother. Her tears at leaving her mother. Driving in the night. In that car. Her head confusedly sifting previous dream of fleeing and the actual in the car of that night. Her mother. She had arms which had caressed her own arms and legs which her own little legs ran after and hands which she had many times hurried to reach and grab. She was her mother. And as she looked back, his reaction at her very understandable sorrow at leaving her mama had made her fear him even more, had driven her further inside—the angry silence with which he answered her sorrow-filled lack.

Besides, she knew she was too much for him. That her past with her mother she could never make right.

The Baker. There he stood in the kitchen. That Baker. That man.

Can I just say

He approached slowly and from the doorway saw her eyes shut closed as he walked in and then stood over her bed; she was so close to sleep, just falling in, but he had to tell her how he felt. He was so happy, these days. Soon the babies would come and he had to tell her, so he sat down at her feet and leaned in toward her as he began his speech: I know you need your sleep, sweet Mara, but can I just say you looked so lovely today, your eyes fierce and shining as you raved about your walk and those green grass fields littered with wildflowers and then also the pretty wood houses and the one with the beautiful garden where you picked the yellow rose that grew right by the sidewalk, afraid it's rightful owner could see you out the window and would yell out so that you rushed in your grabbing and pricked your sweet finger near its tip. And when you showed it to me, your little pricked finger, before you placed the flower in a glass of water I was overwhelmed by your eyes, wild and shining, and your face, flushed so red, so that I could not hold back and rushed to kiss you, your tiny hand, but you drew it quickly away and took a sip of water from the glass that was your vase, sharing water with your rose. You go so fast to girlish shyness and are so easily embarrassed, but this only makes me love you even more. And then as you dropped the flower in the water you said we should have a real vase: Every house needs at least one pretty glass vase, you said in your singsong excitable way. And I saw your newfound happiness there in that statement, your thinking of our home, consideration of details with which to make it right.

Your face so flushed much of the time, and though I know the doctor says it's all the extra blood you're making for the babies, the science so exact, to me it is just pink cheeks and a beautiful vivid glowing you. I love you, Mara. I've been so scared and too sad to say it, but I love you and I'm overjoyed you are not unhappy any longer, that you sing songs with the radio, and that you go on long walks. I love you, Mara, and your belly: I will share it, your belly my belly, my babies too now. And we will start anew and make all those sad grey days right and shining here in California and I know that with my love and your singing and your sweet smile we can make it all alright.

She lay pretending to be sleeping. He'd snuck into her bedroom, in her private time of thinking of her life; she always went to bed right after dinner; he'd cook and she'd help to clean up now, slow because of all the weight, and then exhausted, really, she went to bed where she lay for hours before sleep each night playing and re-playing and then imagining into, her own life. Exhaustion did not mean that sleep came easy when there was so much to think about, so many things to work out. There was a lot to do now. The babies would come soon and she had to figure it all out, all of it. She had to make sense of how she was going to have these babies, think of how to make things different, really different, in their lives. She knew her mother was no kind of mother, a mother she would never be was her mother, but that meant that she would have to get something: something hard and real to put in place of all that. So she had to think all of the time. She had to make it all right. There was so much to sort through and move in and out of and figure out, all before she had the babies. Before she had them she had to have it all clearly figured out. She could not make mistakes. There was no room for any more wrong steps because her life till now had been one great big long mistake. How was she going to go on? She had to think and figure out how she could proceed. And tonight he'd snuck into the bedroom and sat down at her feet and she had quickly closed her eyes to pretend at sleep though nevertheless he had started to talk and talk and talk.

Shut up, she wanted to say. He had intruded. This was her place, her bed, her time. And now he was filling up the room with his chatter, like always he was filling everything up with himself and his needs and his desire, and none of it, none, really had anything to do with her. But here he was going on about flowers and her babies and he was reaching toward her and then drawing back and it was only in his moments of drawing back that she felt anything at all. Relief. I have to figure it all out, she wanted to yell. Stop all your yapping; I have to figure it all out!

I feel faint, sometimes, is what she did say, eyes still closed. I feel dizzy and faint and so I walk and walk and this somehow makes me feel better.

It's the babies, he whispered. It's all of that extra weight, the extra blood, he added, becoming scientific too now—a good firm stance. It's normal, he said quiet.

No, it's not, she wanted to say. It's not normal. I feel faint, barely there. I see things. When I go on my walks I see things, people. And I'm afraid that if I slip, if I let myself actually go, even for a moment, then my life, all of it, will end. I have to stay alert and working and walking. I have to go to the fields even if they scare me. And then I have to think and figure it all out. I need my time; I need to be alone to work it all out, clear it all up, plan it all out, she wanted to say.

I'm tired, is what she did say. I think I need to sleep.

You should do something nice for yourself tomorrow, he said; and here he touched her feet. Go and get a massage. I know a place

I can drive you to. You know, Ivan's wife does, gets them all the time. Or go get your hair cut. That'll make you feel better. Ivan's wife just got hers cut, and dyed. She's like new, like a movie star, Ivan says.

I'm tired, she repeated, pulling herself away. I think I need some sleep. She wanted to say, as she rolled over, that she didn't care about Ivan's wife. She'd never even seen Ivan's wife. Who was that woman to her? And there was no way she would ever let anybody give her a massage. And her mother was the only person who had ever cut her hair. I'm very tired, she repeated.

And then she thanked the ceiling, slowly opened her fierce eyes and audibly thanked the door too as he slipped quiet out the room.

Very pretty

Your hair is very pretty. Muy bonito, the Englishman said.

Today she had walked far. She was thinking of the twins, telling her belly all the things they'd learn at school, convincing them it would be good. That she'd be good; that she'd know how to help them do what they should do. Of course she could not tell them that she had hated school, had always felt miserable and lonely there, had wandered near edges—of classrooms and playgrounds and lunch rooms, the library—wondering how the other kids saw her while pretending to look down at a book, or kicking around some pebbles, or stirring at her disgusting never to be eaten school stew. *If* the other kids saw her at all. The shadow ghost. The there and not there one.

But they would have each other, the twins. They would never be alone. Would never run the risk of simply disappearing.

She stopped short before she reached the next corner. Since seeing her mother she had avoided sleep in all fields and stayed on the sidewalks instead. She had been walking for almost an hour today and when she lifted her head she saw a restaurant there. She had never wandered to the part of town where the houses stopped and the restaurants and shops began. Los Angeles wasn't like Mexico City where homes and businesses shared almost every block. A candy and soda shop to which you could run and fetch your mother's cigarettes, at least, at the end of every block. Here it was a series of neighborhoods, little towns each, full of houses and those open fields for sometimes two or three miles before you saw any shops at all. But then, suddenly, out of nowhere there was a restaurant. And a toy store. And a pharmacy and soda shop. And right across the street from all of this was a hair salon. She thought of the baker in her room last night, talking and talking, forcing her out of her own thoughts, as she looked at the row of hair dryers, all but one vacant, that woman sitting with eyes closed, maybe even quite asleep. She imagined that woman as Ivan's wife, her chest gently rising and falling with each breath, fingers on her stomach loosely intertwined. The anger she had felt in the darkness, the desperation at his not leaving, was all that there had been for her as he'd talked into the night. But today, in the bright light of day, she thought that maybe he'd been right.

She was so nervous lately. The walking was no longer enough. It was clear that that was no way to solve it. She had to do something real. Maybe if what she wanted was to be different from her mother, maybe if what she wanted was to leave the past behind, maybe one way to begin was by letting someone else cut off all her hair. Maybe being pulled out of her own head was not such a bad thing. She should *do* something. Being in there all of the time was making her more and more nervous. To keep from going crazy maybe all she needed was to cut off all her hair. Maybe if she started doing things, changing the outside, the inside would have to change too. Then she wouldn't have to think so much. It would just happen. She would know what she had to do, how, from now on, she had to act. And if she acted happy then she could be happy and if she were happy she could make a new life. For herself. For the babies.

She inched up to the window and peeked in from its side. She saw the man, young, his hair dark blonde, cutting an older woman's hair. She saw him lean down and say something into her ear, saw that woman laugh a great big laugh in response, and his beaming—

eyebrows arched and eyes shining now—at the woman through the mirror, the looking glass. The other side.

I want to cut my hair, she said that night, as she picked up the plates and he swept. I think you're right. I need to do something. I need to cut my hair all off.

How old are you?
Seventeen.
Well, now you look seventeen. You look like a woman. When your baby comes you will look like a woman, instead of a little girl yourself.

She looked at him through the mirror. He had his hands, eyeliner tube still in the right one, resting on her shoulders. Her hair a teased short bob, eyes dramatic with the liner he'd applied. And he held her big-eyed cat-like gaze. Her eyes dropped and she smiled slyly as she slipped out from under his grip before sliding out of the chair.

All the way home she thought of their talk. An Englishman. When she'd sat down at his chair he'd reached down from where he stood at her back, had gently lifted all of her hair and removed the thin gold chain which her mother had given her as a girl and which she had never taken off; small and tight it fit now, like a choker. He'd swept his hands under her hair, undone it, and then through the mirror held her eyes as he moved his right hand, brushing her jaw with his fingertips, in front of her chest where he let drop the tiny gold chain into her awkwardly raised and slowly unfurled hand. That done, he began to cut. He loved LA, he said, because the women were so beautiful here. The Mexican girls and their olive skin and thick dark hair. Their slow and sultry walk. He and his English friends had never seen anything like them in their small English towns. And the middle-aged white women flirted and gave good tips. He had smiled and laughed as he told her all this. I ask girls out all the time. And she had not been offended but had laughed because he laughed and it had felt so good to be around someone who laughed. She understood most of what he said, thank god for her in English radio and tv. And he spoke a little bit of Spanish for his love of the Mexican girls. Muñeca, he called her. And so there was this back and forth dance of the two languages, each of them forgiving the other's lingual mistakes.

Muy bonito, he had said of her long hair. Muy muy bonita, he said once it was all cut. Now we can see the rest of you, Muñeca.

Cut it short, she had said, and then she mentioned *My Life to Live*, and the one English film she had seen at her Mexico City movie theater, *A Taste of Honey*, and he'd looked up, surprised.

So, you've seen that? he asked in his accent.

Yes, she replied in her accent. The two of them so obviously not from here having a conversation about a film that they both thought was them, she because of the subject matter—a pregnant young girl with a wicked mother and an outsider boyfriend; and he because of history and geography and a crush on Rita Tushingham.

You want hair like Rita? he asked.

Yes, she answered, proud that she knew things now.

And then in three long swipes he cut it all off, before leaning in in a more concentrated fashion to mold and snip and make right. And then, her dark short-banged hair now framing her face, he'd told her to sit still as he applied the liner to her eyes.

There, now you are Rita and Anna both, he said as the same horns that Manuel had brought on many of his nights piped out overhead.

Miles, she said.

Yes, he'd answered.

Baker, baker, not the baker

Now she had a here and now. Now she was no longer just in the past of sad and disappointed fury at her mother or the hopeful future of transformation through the love of coming little twins. Now there was a hairdresser who laughed and cut and made her laugh. And he'd given her beautiful dramatic life-searching eyes. She practiced her looks in front of the mirror. Like a movie star. She kissed the mirror. She pursed her lips and looked coyly down like Anna Karina in that close-up right before her eyes both fill with tears.

Now she had a here and now, something drawing her to and invigorating her here and now. She saw him there before her, scissors cutting all her ties to mournful past. Snip. And his deep-set staring blue eyes.

She sees him there before her and as he cuts the hair away from her neck he reaches his mouth down and sucks her sorrow right out, slowly inching down her spine. The hairdresser—opening her up with his tongue, bringing her out of her head and onto the surface of her own skin with that tongue. And she lies down on her bed and forgets her mother and the babies, as this man disguised as her hand heals all her wounds with scissors and tongue.

It was impossible to leave the in front of the mirror and flat on her back daydreams for the babies were making it so hard to walk. She was starting to feel the weight of her babies—the shortness of breath caused by the mass of her babies, their actuality, by their pressing into lungs and heart—now for the first time. And, besides, when she did walk she looked funny. Like a big bellied cowboy, skinny legs and arms.

And so she mostly sat here, in her own bedroom, and, often, after she thought of the hairdresser, she ate the baker's treats, especially the custard filled ones. She brought them to her bed and she sat back on stacked pillows as she ate with real hunger, and while she again thought of the hairdresser she slurped at the baker's custard insides. She ate instead of walking, though the doctor told her to start moving again to prepare for the long push and pull night.

But now there was only one place to which she wanted to walk and so she mostly didn't because besides being so tired what do you say to a hairdresser when you aren't there for him to cut off your hair? When what you want is for him to cut off your past. She had made it there once, to the across the street almost there possibilities of the here and now, before her racing heart asked her to turn around and inch her way slowly back, ridiculous belly, like an independent being leading her home. And then she got half way there two other times, before on the third attempt her water broke and ran all down her legs. The pain started quickly, within half an hour, and when she finally made it back crying more from the frustration than anything else, she laid down with legs slightly spread there on the couch before the baker, not the hairdresser like she dreamt of, but the baker, made it home from the restaurant.

It was six months after the babies were born that she left the sleeping two there in their bassinet, with the baker looking quizzically at her as she said she needed a few moments alone; she needed to go for a walk. It was six months after those two were born that she walked through those now familiar streets, heart in her mouth, breathing heavy the whole way as she went back to see if the real hairdresser would kiss her as passionately as her closed eyes bedroom one daily had.

A taste of...

This hairdresser was not shy. He had seen the same movies as Manuel. He listened to some of the same music as Manuel. But there, she soon found, was the end of the match.

Wait, he had said when she entered, approached, stood staring as he asked if she'd come in to trim those bangs.

No, she'd said; where did her bravery come from? She could never summon up from where this determination had come. No, she'd repeated as she looked, directly now like a daring French girl in a film, into his eyes.

Wait a few minutes, he had replied.

In half an hour he was done with the old woman; he led her to the register, smiling and with his arm around her shoulder, and then he silently took Mara outside. Within five minutes he had his hand on her belly, All gone?, it wandered to the back of her neck where it rested, cool, before she replied with a nod, and then, her breath having fully stopped, he pulled her face up at an angle to his. And Mara melted from the inside.

Now, Seventeen, where is your baby?

Home. The baby's home. And that was the only time, on that first day, that this twenty-seven year old man asked. He took her hand and walked her to his car, opened the door for her, got in his side, then drove her three blocks down, under the partial shade of an old oak tree. And his breathing on her neck drove her crazy, his mouth inching up and down her dappled arms.

And when she left that day, they'd determined, without saying so much, that she'd be coming back, every day, at the same early afternoon time.

And for the next half year this is when she was the happiest. This is when she felt alive. The rest of the time she was nervous. Her heart raced the rest of the time. Often she would start weeping from pure exhaustion. Sometimes it felt as if her breath would fully stop. But in his presence she slowed down, felt herself actual, there, physically, before him. When he touched her she felt herself bodily there, felt her neck and her arms. She felt her lips and her upper thighs. Felt the merging together of all her insides. When he whispered she leaned in to hear his animal hush. And when he laughed he made her laugh.

At home with the babies she was anxious. She was scattered. She'd be reaching for one, and the other would start wailing, no warning, a piercing cry. Her heart raced. She couldn't calm even one, for if one was crying the other soon began. She was lost in the need of their mouths. She would pet and pet their heads when they finally fell asleep, their brown fuzz, for long periods without focus, without realizing the passage of time. They would awaken and she'd grasp it had been hours she'd been petting them, hours they had napped and in which she could have laid herself down, instead of standing, mechanical and blind. She did diaper and sometimes successfully rock one at a time and once in a while even sang, though not ever fully present, eyes staring straight most of the time.

And the baker made her crazy. His lulling the babies to sleep with no effort. His bouncing them at the same time in his crossed arms, and then setting them gently down one by one. The way he could give them both the bottle, coo at them so they both smiled back or stare deep into their eager eyes. She would watch him do these things, upon getting home at three o'clock, and it was a relief, but it also made her furious, his overly beaming pride. Those were her babies. And even if she was partially lost in the not enough of her and the too much of them, Mona and Manuel were not his.

Though he claimed each breakthrough as a personal victory. When they sat up, when they began to crawl. He was so loud. Hooting and cheering. The way he clapped and yelled out to them to encourage them to walk.

They're too little, she said from her chair. It's not good for their legs. But he did not seem to hear, kneeling there before them, clapping his hands together as they inched toward him with wide eyes.

He didn't even notice that her walks took longer and longer. He never even asked.

The hairdresser, his name was Michael—another M name, and she saw this as a sign—and his hair fell down and into his soulful sunken deep blue eyes; Michael made her feel her body for the first time. It was not just a longing like she'd felt for Manuel, it was that, a longing, but every day it was satisfied.

Within a few months he was saying, Let's go to London. My friend is opening a salon there; I'm making plans. Remember that the past is always past. You and I can go to London. You don't love him, and we can bring the baby. We'll bring your little one.

This one

This night. Not this night. A choice. It was as simple as that.

She thought of the ghost-girl who had come out of nowhere to pick up the apple with the worm in it which she had only just dropped; that girl and she were one. She thought of her mother, a child then, feeding innocent little grasshoppers to the spiders that lived in the garden wall recesses and cracks. But no, it had not just been her mother. It had been her, hunting down the unsuspecting insects, and each time, with Bibi, sharing in the shriek of morbid delight. What was there inside her that had made her so willingly do that, fall prey to that kind of pleasure? She was her mother. And her mother was Bibi. And Bibi and she were both fatherless ones. Her mother the pander. And she was the apprentice to all of that. She had never felt safe, had always felt like the kind of girl whom an angel would let fall through the slats. A pulling back of the hand at the critical moment. And she had been the pander, no, the apprentice in all of that.

She thought of the woods there outside Mexico City. She and the baker had approached them in the twilight. She had never been to the woods before, never even knew there were woods to the north of the city. It was confusing to her, all those trees. It got dark quickly as they entered so that it was night before it was really night. And then she'd stayed in them, those woods, for that's when his insults on her mother began. That's when the barrage of distaste had begun. And in the turning away of her face, in the sudden distrust of the baker, the darkness had descended down and deep into her life. Quick like she had always been already waiting for the darkness, for the misery, to drop. And now with Michael she felt herself, finally, leaving those woods. She must leave them behind. Leave that twilight which had changed so quickly to dark and uncertainty. Into black night. Leave the dark shadow of her past. Leave it all behind.

Sitting on the curb, waiting for him to come, she'd lifted her head to the sky. And he'd come, almost like she'd made him up, a dream actualized, coasting to her in his black Chevelle, and she'd hopped in departing those tall grass mad fields and her mother's shadow, her grandmother's garden and the depth of those dark woods; her tight skirt black, a scarf tied around her head, sunglasses covering her eyes, they'd driven to under the dappled light of the big oak tree. He'd pulled off her dark glasses and thrown them on the dash and then kissed her as with one hand he removed her scarf and her breathing had quickened, and as he ate her lips he told her that now he was really going; her heart stopped as he told her that his friend in London had finally opened his salon. But then he'd said: why don't we go away? Like the lyrics of a silly love song. Why don't you come with me? Wouldn't it be nice to live together in the kind of world where we belong? You know its gonna make it that much better when we can say goodnight and stay together. Wouldn't it be nice if we could wake up in the morning when the day is new? And after having spent the day together hold each other close the whole night through. Happy times together we've been spending. I wish that every kiss was never ending....

She had never told him there were two. And that was not like a silly love song. She'd exed one out. He had assumed the one, and she had never said: No, there are two. Your baby, he had said, and had instantly sealed it with that; why had she not explained then? What was it that had made her stop from telling him that they were twins, what was it that had made her lie like that; complicit; the apprentice; and when finally directly asked for details she had maybe stuttered for a moment but then had quickly and so effortlessly recovered and simply said it was a boy. Manuel. My baby is a boy.

In fact, she had not told him much. Because there was something about having told the baker so many many things, there was something about not having been able to stop her tongue once it had started that had made her misery more real, so she had not told the hairdresser much of anything at all. And he had not asked. As if they had signed some kind of silent pact. Which was fine because she did not want to live this life here under the big oak tree, with all of that old life jumbled in. She wanted this to be this. And so, no, there could not be much of that. Diluting and infecting. Mixing in and affecting. And when the under the old oak tree began to expand out, into the larger world beyond his mouth on her body in his car, she still did not tell him much. With Manuel she had been awed. With the baker overwhelming and too much; with him she could feel and laugh and leave her past her past.

So she just told him that this man, she did not love him. And she was not a wife. He was a man and she just a girl and she did not love him. In fact, he had tricked her. And though he was kind to the baby, took good care of the baby, she did not love him.

Well, you can't live without love, the scissor man whispered in her ear. Then he spoke in more lyrics from another pop song. Disconnected and passionate. I don't care what they say; I won't stay in a world without love. And that suited her just fine. Won't stay in a world without love.... Through the window her stare, on her stomach and her arm the dappled light.

I won't stay in a world without love, and his hand slipped deep between her thighs.

So on this night, this baby. Not this baby. In his mind there was only one. And so there was only one; so much easier to carry only one when you steal away, weeping, into the dark yet vaguely hopeful night.

2:
How death befell me

(Los Angeles, 1997)

The dead father

walked numb, plodding feet, the hospital halls a maze, the treat at the end of it: my purple-hued father. Sometimes, if I was particularly tired or in a low mood, I would walk into the massive building through one of the countless other doors, pick and choose, go up and down elevators a bit, wanting to get lost for a while. I even ended up at the wrong set of rooms a few times, other people's fathers, but back tracked, of course, dutiful daughter, started again. And there he'd inevitably be, the stock-still endpoint: my dad. Though I never quite got used to it.

For a month now, each day as if it were the first time, my heart had palpitated and my breathing had nearly stopped as I reached that doorway and was met with the sight of my increasingly weakened vaguely mauve father, laid out and now one with countless existence machines. I'd push myself forward and then: Hi, I would say, sit at his feet.

Hi, he'd breathe back, faint smile at his lips.

I have heard that this happens. I know it does. I do. So it should not have come as such a shock when he did it, for people do this; just as they're going they empty themselves. Their burden your burden now. You must decide if their unfinished business is worth taking on. Yet it caught me terribly off guard; and it would be an understatement to say that for me it seemed like too much, that I didn't want all his loose ends. That what I wanted, all I wanted, was to blank myself out. Swim below the surface for a while. Sleep a deep sleep and then, on occasionally waking, move ever so slow, hands reaching out for support, eyes heavy from the slumber just left and nodding already toward that soon to come.

Though at some wakeful level I knew too that his stuff was my stuff. That it's the nature of nature that a parent is you.

"I couldn't do it," he said. "I couldn't keep two. Reach into my pocket," he said, and I didn't. "Reach into my pocket," he said; and that time I did.

I slipped the letter from out of his shirtfront, and when I lifted my gaze to his eyes again, my father was dead.

The search

After my mother died there was no searching. He'd never spoken it, had never made the attempt at clearing things up, and I tried only once, to make some sense of that death. My heart rushing faster at the sight of him, sweat rising, though I worked hard at steadying myself, looking mature, composed, ready for the information; I walked into the kitchen and asked questions, big and general, nothing too close, too specific:

"What happened?"

"I don't know," he said, reluctantly turning to face me.

"What did they say?"

"Nothing. They had no idea. She was gone and I was distraught and there was you. And besides, nobody questioned doctors in those days."

"How soon after me? How could she die just like that? Hearts don't just stop."

"They do. Hers did," he said near a whisper now and there was something terrifying in his barely there voice.

"Papa?"

And my father's desperation suddenly rose, "I don't know. I don't know!" I tore my eyes from his and focused on his hands which were now visibly shaking.

"How? How do you not know?" I wanted to yell, inch up to his face and scream it until I got an answer, but I feared that I would kill him; life seemed that tenuous to me, my guilt in death that clear. So instead I took it as a given, pulled my eyes away and dropped the questions. Ran out weeping with my little dog behind me.

It was lucky, then, that after what had happened that day everyone at school dropped their questions too. From then on they mostly saw me as a freak, someone to be wary of, and this was fine with me for it meant I didn't have to reach any deeper, bring it up once more. I could fall into my silence again for they all knew not to say a word.

I think I was twelve or thirteen. Eleven, fourteen. I believe a classmate had said something. Perhaps this girl, Angie may have been her name, was beautiful, which would have made it even worse, her long legs and red always softly parted lips. She rarely looked at you when she spoke and the whole school lived in awe of her casual coldness. Yet, somehow, she'd focused on me and though I suspected it was only because she was fighting with her group of friends, her attention was thrilling.

I should have known, should have been able to see it would lead to bad things, for I was not the same kind; I hunched and I plodded, was excitable and nervous and awkward and shy. My hands never rested. My heart raced wildly when I was called on in class. My best friend was the Japanese girl, Mineko, who had a quiet and wicked sense of humor but whose overly firm mother still clothed her in fru fru dresses, patent leather shoes and frilly socks. She would tell me stories about an uncle, her mother's brother, which made me shudder even then. Those slowly raised little girl full-skirted frocks.

There we are, me and Mineko, hiding in one corner of the large field. She's calling the other kids names, idiots and savages and I look on from under the veil of dread she is putting voice to.

There we are, at the courtyard eating a ridiculous school sanctioned lunch of Hostess and Frito Lay and Coca-cola when Angie and five of her reedy and barely dressed friends come floating down the hall; she is back in with them and they are smiling and talking amongst themselves, unconcerned with the rest of us—though her eyes did flash at me and lock with mine in a moment of mutual terror, for we'd shared something real, those minutes of terrifying violence had cracked through our separate adolescent veneers—a pack of mid-riff tops and mini-skirts and skin-tight lycra-laced pants, so much indifferent flesh; they seemed dirty and challenging and pristinely unapproachably clean at the same time. We were from two separate worlds, inhabited whole different schools, them and us.

Yet, somehow, a few days back I'd been at her house, a shockingly shabby little house, not much larger than ours where Angie lived with three older brothers and a mother. No one was home. We went into the room she shared with her mother and pulled open the drawer where in a huge and seething pile all of their make-up was kept and then Angie placed me in front of the mirror and she began to brush my hair, "Like this," she said, "you should part it on the side."

Her hand on my head. Cool and easy and able, while my breath caught deep inside my chest.

We applied lipstick and eyeliner, put Bow Wow Wow on the turntable and then went outside where I worked hard to be casual, forced myself to lighten up, move my body with fake ease as Angie taught me how to smoke a cigarette. I didn't get it, just sucked into my mouth and then out, but Angie could make the smoke come out her nose. She threw her head back and laughed loud all afternoon, and I laughed too, speeding forward with the music even when I didn't quite understand what had been so great, what had been so hilariously funny.

It was hot and Angie told me to put on one of her cut-off black t-shirts, and although I felt naked, we walked onto the street like that.

Up the street to a burger stand and I worked hard at avoiding the eyes of anyone driving by, all those passing cars, silent drivers and their obsequious passengers who must be shocked by the sight of me in cut off shirt and lipstick, my hair parted callingly to one side.

We each ordered a shake and we split an order of fries and then Angie pulled out another cigarette and though I did not want any I took it and with Annabella's Eiffel Tower running through my spine pretended to inhale it once or twice.

And then two boys came riding up on tiny mountain bikes and they mumbled hello to Angie and one of them asked who I was. Angie said I was her best friend and what were they stupid standing and staring like that. She looked away from them and up at the sky and then the one boy, John, beautiful deep-set green eyes, told us to go to the park the next day. He told Angie to make sure and bring her best friend. Without looking at him Angie said maybe, she would think about it. And then the boys went riding off. Idiots, she said after they'd left.

His eyes, though; beautiful hands. Long arms shining with the sweat, sparkling in the sun.

I put a napkin in my pants' pocket before we started the walk home.

At my door I crouched and wiped at the lipstick on my face, pulled down on the shirt that ended well above my belly button, then marched fast and straight into the bathroom, past my father who had his back turned in the kitchen. And then I stood in front of that mirror where I looked at myself for four, or twenty, minutes. Until Blinker yelped and drew me outside of myself. I washed my face then, and opened the door, bent over and patted and patted at her little head, kissed between her eyes, my long hair an umbrella that joined and made us one.

The next day we walked to the park and lay down in the grass and looked up at the sky that had some very pretty big white clouds in it. We were lying there, like this and this was all I really needed, this quiet here with my best friend. This warmth of the air and coolness of the grass and the sound of our soft breathing mingling back and forth. And then two bikes came skidding over, on top of us now, and we leapt, our breath catching, and Angie was immediately screaming, "What are you a retard or something? You could of killed us." And John didn't answer but looked over at me and I thought of the bright red with which I had again colored my lips, and then I felt a warmth grow up and spread inside me. And when I looked over Angie was wiping at some dirt that the boys had sent flying over and onto her arm.

"Yeah. I'm a retard. That's why you dig me." And Angie stood herself up and John, laughing and slightly awkward, rode over, bent towards her and gave her a kiss on her coolly offered cheek.

And my heart begged for home from deep within.

But I couldn't move because Angie whom I immediately understood had seen John looking at me was now saying something awful, my mother: *You know, Mona, my mother says your mother...* in front of those two. For a moment I was terrified, wanted to run, though my legs wouldn't budge, but instantly it rose up inside me and I turned sudden and hit her, slapped her in the face and then leapt with hands open, grabbed at her hair and didn't let go. I think there was screaming, crying, and then the boys were pulling me away, clumps of disengaged hair in my still clutching hands, my mouth clenched, tears held in.

And when I got home my heart was still racing, and there he was in the kitchen baking, so calm, happy, serene, so outside of everything, life for him just flour and eggs; and I wanted to hurt him. I wanted my father to weep.

How, how do you not know anything? I wanted to yell.

Though, of course, when his hands began shaking, I couldn't keep going; my anger could kill him, I knew. *I don't know*, he'd repeated and I pulled out of it all. Took it off like a coat. I walked into my room and sat at my desk, my small dog, Blinker, at my legs. And then this question that I had not intended to think, that I never again wanted to bring up, was mostly just gone. I settled on my father's explanation: Mother dead in childbirth, and the nineteenth century brutality of it I once again grew accustomed to, a fully sealed package once more; and until recently it had been nearly thirty years of a distant vaguely aching fact—only lightly tinged with gnawing doubt.

Until recently, of course, because just a few weeks ago he himself had brought it up, opened it up again when he abruptly turned from the hanging tv in his hospital room and in a flat low voice told me she had been there, *that she had been there*, not dead, for a full year before her heart stopped. He looked away from me and at the wall in front of him now, past that tv, confusion written on his face: Maybe not quite a full year, he amended... no, it was more, a year and two months... in the middle of the night... or, no, he recalled now that he'd come home from work, his chef's hat still on his head for some odd reason... he could see it all now, she all laid out... just like that. His hand swept out in front of him while all jumbled and vague my father's face struggled a moment further before he stopped short and turned his head away to look out the window. And then he mumbled something about it seeming much easier, clearer, less painful, less complicated to explain the loss to me by saying she'd never been with me at all. That when I was four or five and had first asked, he'd turned and looked long and hard at the tiny me and those words are what had come out, death in childbirth, so final, clear, extreme; no need to add any further information with something so defined. He was terrified of the serious little figure standing in front of him, he admitted now, all that I might with my grave questions bring up.

And there had been a brother too, he went on, a twin. And he was out there, still, somewhere.

When my father first told me all this it seemed so abstract I could bear it. I could. It paled, somehow, at that moment, to him, big and actual, there, on the hospital bed, the penitent. He had given my brother up (in that nineteenth century way) he said, because he was convinced he could not have two. He was overcome by my mother's death and could not ever have taken care of the both. He had felt the son would fare better in the world without his father than the daughter could. Plus, he felt he would somehow be a better father for a girl. He was a late twentieth century man, soft and gentle. Unsure of his manliness, of his need of anything he could refer to as his manliness. He didn't know how to throw balls around with a young boy.

Yes, I said, my ears faintly ringing. For all of this, all of his excuses—and in the two weeks before his death I heard many more than just these three, spilling out of his large sloppy lips in a rapid liquid stream as he laid there, flat and immobile on that narrow bed—were just guilty reasoning after the fact, that I knew. Nevertheless, the excuses bubbled and splattered out of him and it was as if he wanted them to lift him up off of that bed so that he could float away and into death on a river of his own vague reasons: the murky whys, the silty whys, flowing opaque whys.

But I had known, as I sat there as confessor, that none of what he said was really it. Nevertheless, I would rub at his feet and nod, consoling: Yes. I know. I know, I would say, my hands strongly kneading through thin hospital sheet. Though the only thing I really knew for certain was that there couldn't be a reason. How to justify the choice? He had probably just tossed a coin: heads girl, tails boy. I know this, for I too have often thus used chance to quell bad conscience.

And all of that I could live with, lost brother, absent mother; but this, now, the dead father at the dawn of the twenty-first century. This was too much. What would I do without him?

Though I have to admit that soon after he told me about them, when I wasn't with him, I began to try to call them up, for she had been there for a year; I went home after every long hospital visit of his final weeks and while laying on my bed for hours at a time concentrated hard and tried to get back to the one year old me, surrounded by people, my mother and my father, a brother.

But I couldn't. I could only draw myself up alone, my father lurking in the shadowed wings.

And then I worked hard to imagine how he had done it: tried to draw up a picture of the discomfited young man with the tiny boy bundled in his arms, all wrapped up in fanciful blankets. The gentle if ill-at-ease father walking from his parked car (if I set it in the 1800's it would have to be a carriage) to the front doors of the stark white modernist building. I come in close and read the sign: Lil' Bit Adoption Agency: unwanted children wanted. From this angle I can see the tears streaming down his face when he runs back out of the building; and then as he drives away the sobs that catch him up so that he has to pull over at the side of the road for quite a long while, a man with no son now; I go inside his head then and try to decide for myself whether the father, at his deepest and most true self, felt it was actually and absolutely a necessary thing, this giving away, or if he'd just convinced himself at the surface, with a toxic mix of convoluted and illogical arguments that always ended with: it will be better for all of us—especially the boy.

I watch, then, as he turns his eyes away from her while he hands some bundled up bills to the buck-toothed teen-age girl whom he has paid to watch the baby me for the three hours he was out. She grabs at the money with the same two grimy fingers that not an hour before had disdainfully pinched me when I began crying because she had missed my mealtime; it seems that the baby-sitter had forgotten to keep track of the hour as she had become rather involved in giving her boyfriend a handjob in the front room where my little playpen sat. It seems my hungry whimpering was distracting him and keeping him from finishing so that she stopped for a second, reached out with angry sweaty fingers, and pinched. It seems my now louder shrieks had the opposite effect of the whimpering, and her paramour was, with the aid of my wailing voice, able to accomplish his task. My first threesome. This boy stole a guilty glance in my direction as he buttoned his jeans; he then awkwardly patted Fifi on the back, hastily thanked her, and rushed out the front door.

Fifi, the baby-sitter, would run out the same front door only 45 minutes later, after grabbing her fee from my father's hands, and leave us there alone, father and daughter. Father would see the lingering redness in my eyes and conclude that I had been crying not as a result of the soggy pinch but, rather, at the same thing he had been shedding water over, the loss of the boy. And then with his own red eyes I can see him look directly into mine as he lifts me out from the little playpen, holds me up close to his weary face and then almost drops me when his heart runs ahead of him, jumps, and then stops for just one second.

Perhaps I can not handle even one, he says.

And I begin shrieking in renewed awareness of my hunger.

Clearly, my anger at his lies began to build slowly over those following weeks, yet I said nothing to him, and accepted the mission, the search for the lost one, the twin brother. My father's burden in fact my burden now. "When you find him you must give him this letter from me," he had whispered as my fingers touched the envelope, "his one true father."

I looked hard into his eyes, suspicious of everything he said now. But then I nodded.

If nothing else, this filial obligation provided me with something to do, something to fill up the time until I could remember how to pull up from down below, remember how to walk awake, remember how to breathe.

Gather up and go

I live on top of a mountain. Of course, it is not really a mountain, but it is more than a hill. It's got Mount in the name and this makes it almost obligatory to refer to it as a mountain, this little suburb, Mount W., once an artist enclave of shacks and little dilapidated craftsmen houses and half a dozen modernist ones. There are many open lots and much overgrowth, and countless neighbors who keep inoperable old cars and other trash heaps in their driveways; an inexpensive place to buy a house is what it was to my father. It is not kept up and manicured the way so many of the residential areas of this city are, but it is not a ghetto either, is just north of downtown, though you'd never know it was here unless you had a reason to come up its little winding roads. There are numerous trails I've never wandered. The grounds of a large yogi church down the road. And now, after more than a month of his absence, it was him and me on the mountain again, as it had always been.

I'd felt too nervous to drive so I had taken the train and now, on our return, I got us off at the foot of the hill. I had picked the unadorned box, brass, had them pour him into that, and after he had been handed in it back to me I walked out of there and placed him in a large canvas bag in which I carried him onto this train. And now I was lugging him back up the big hill to our little house, heavy, talking to him the whole way, as when he was still alive, for

I had always done most of the talking. And, as I made our way inside the house I found the strength to say things I had not before been able to voice: "How could you never have mentioned him? My brother a blank? If you had just been a bit tougher, accepted the challenge, kept the two, dealt with your fate, then I wouldn't have to do this now, make up for you now" I said as I walked into his room. "Your weakness has always been my curse," I added in some anger, finally able to put succinctly something that I had felt to be true my whole life, though I stopped myself from going further, from mentioning my mother, while I boosted him onto the dresser, wiped away the fingerprints.

And then all my withheld anger, years and years and years of it, made me angrier still, for why should I, the daughter, always be put in the position of being angry at him, the father, his weakness, even in his death. And worse: why should I continue to live in fear that my fury would hurt him, kill him, even when he was already dead?

I calmed myself down with one whiskey and twenty-five cigarettes while I sat in our mess of a living room and stared straight for what felt like days.

When I was able to move again I rummaged through the house, the piles of junk, looking for things to bring with me on my voyage. I would need a satchel, some gingham fabric tied into a little hobo pack full of my belongings, and some biscuits for the trip…

And when I had finished my packing I drank a big glass of milk to settle my churning stomach and went to bed. The next morning I would set off on my way.

It was bright and early, as I was walking through the door, one foot already over that threshold, that I decided I should do something more, something special and rife with meaning before I set off on this search. I should wear different clothing, beautiful and distinct, to mark the occasion, should read one more book, garner wisdom from somewhere. Eat a good hearty meal. Have one more night's rest in my own bed. So I walked back over that doorway, into the small craftsman house, and dug about in my closet. There was nothing I wanted to change into, just endless variations on the black skirt and sweater that are like a uniform for me. I walked into the bathroom and looked around there too. I pulled back my hair, inspected myself and thought about cutting. Too clichéd I decided; how many women have cut theirs all off to mark a turning point? Though I wished I could be dramatic in that way, that I could make a grand gesture, personally significant, without being self-conscious and mocking, me against me. I opened the medicine cabinet, then, not really looking for anything anymore, lost as to what it was I was searching for, and I saw his shaving cream there, shook then sprayed a bit into my hand. An old bottle of alcohol. Blood pressure medicine, his name infinitesimal on the label, and I thought about how those two words made no sense, his first and last name, it should just say Father, or Dad, or Dead.

How had he not ever mentioned a brother? My mother? Can people be blanked out just like that, willed away? How could my father never have said they had been there? A year turned into dust?

I shifted and focused on an ancient box of loose powder, there in the corner, surely not mine. *Gitana*, it said in black lettering on the red box, Gipsy. I had never noticed it before, and I knew, for certain, it was not mine.

I pulled my eyes away, unsure of what that box meant, and saw that tiny bottle next to and almost behind the dusty old plastic container of alcohol: *deep water blue*, it was called. I grabbed it out of the medicine cabinet, forgetting about the shaving cream on my hand so that the little bottle swam in that white mound for a moment before I washed it all away. I removed my shoes, walked to the bed where I sat down and painted each little toenail, holding one digit at a time, rolling it lovingly—which is to say in full and tender concentration—between two fingers to get at the whole thing; I tried then, though it seemed forced even to me (but who else was this for?) to give the whole thing an air of the celebratory... some assumed excitement at what these toenails signaled, my coming venture—affected effect: colorful toes. My personally significant gesture. But it only just worked. Twenty minutes of mild distraction it had barely been. And then I padded around the dirty wood floors, flatfooted so as not to mess the job, my heart rushing forward now, for I really had to leave.

I dropped the tiny bottle in the satchel, and as I walked over to say good-bye to my father it came to me. My hesitation had somehow been tied to leaving him there, venturing forth on my own. But I didn't have to. Who said I had to? I could bring him with me. A letter is one thing, but a father, himself, even as a pile of ashes, even in that desiccated form, that presence would be vastly more significant than a letter could ever be. I'd take my father to him. He'd make the voyage with me and I'd present our father to my brother, so that at least in this way they could meet once more.

Thrilled and invigorated by my resolution, I rushed over, grabbed him up, and placed him on the floor where I worked hard to pry open the thick brass box with a screwdriver. I cut my ring finger a bit with the tip as I finally rammed it open, and then as I poured him into a big Ziploc bag a little of my blood dripped in there with him. This took me aback for it didn't seem right; in fact it gave me the creeps. I thought, then, about how each cell has all of you fully inscribed into it so that if I left my blood in there like that it would be as if I were already dead too. Of course I plunged my hand in then, to try to get myself out, but it was all so sticky that I had to give up; when I pulled out my hand parts of my father were stuck all over it. I stood still, staring at him there for a minute or two, my dad an ash glove, wondering how you're supposed to deal with a mess like that, but in the end I decided there probably was no protocol and just washed him off in the sink. I hoped it would all be okay, that I hadn't somehow sealed my own fate, and then I wrote his name on the white space provided, zipped him up and inspected him like this for awhile before dropping him into my satchel. I then gave the cat one last scratch under the neck, a quick triple pat on his rump, put him out, locked up the house, and once again overjoyed at the fact of his company, set off on my way.

An adventure?

We'd been living in this house since I was four years old. Before that we lived in an even smaller one down the hill and up the freeway a bit, exactly six short exits, in fact. Or four train stops and then a twelve minute walk. That house sat in a long double row of identical tiny houses, the kind of little houses that some people choose to call cottages because it makes their inadequate size sound quaint.

I remember the day we found this house, not in full detail, of course, but in jarring vivid scenes, though nothing really happened to mark that day as significant enough for these earliest memories, nothing other than finding this place. The house seemed sunnier. Light came in the windows. And this was immediately noted as a good thing, for I don't remember light in our previous house. Had there been any windows at all? And there was a hiking trail just down the way, two hundred yards, a fire trail, the realtor told us, and I didn't understand what that meant. Though I got the sense of it being a road used for misfortune, and grew scared... it was so close. We were at the rear of the house, and we stayed on a moment as this woman in her ill fitting power suit, yellow, walked inside again through the back door. I remember turning my gaze from where she'd just stood to look beyond that steep yard, down at the wide street that spread out below us, as a silent group of people walked toward that trail with their dogs. *Where are they going?* I asked my father, anxious at where they were headed for the word "fire" still rang in my mind. But he was not looking in their direction, seemed to be looking up, at the sky. *Away*, he said, and this response terrified me; who was he talking about? So I looked up too, toward the spot he was staring at to try and locate the answer, and then down and back at him, puzzled, *On an adventure. Don't worry; they'll be back*, he continued and then reached down and grabbed at my hand.

But he hadn't turned to look toward them; had he even seen that hushed group walk by? So that I was absolutely not sure who he was talking about then, and this made my heart race so that I pressed hard into his big leg for warmth and comfort, though he was the very one who had unnerved me. But I realize I was only four, and even if I was close to five, this seems too young for an actual memory.

We bought the house. And though I saw people walk down and toward that trail many, many times—more often than not the linen-clad members of that church down the way—it was years before I wandered to the edges of it myself, only now that I was preparing to actually walk on it. *It leads into a forest*, I'd been told by others on the hill, and this very fact which had colluded with my indistinct fear to keep me away before, was what was leading me to it now.

My father and I, when we went out, went to more structured places, nothing so wild as that trail, the park by our old house, more often than not. Picnics, for outings inevitably involved food with us. Sometimes he would chase me after one of his big meals, pretending he could not quite catch me. Me running away fast, at first, my hair flying in the breeze. But then, even when I slowed down, a crawl almost at times, he'd become invariably more sluggish, arms stretched out, though never quite reaching. Finally, I would have to stop and turn and walk back to him, frustrated. *You should try harder sometimes, or it's not any fun*, I remember instructing him once.

Naughty doll

I t was after dinner and I was in my room, was playing with my dolls, had them all lined up and was scolding the whole bunch of them for misbehaving when I heard him, noisy, coming down the hall. This in itself was shocking, my father didn't ever make any noise, so that I began to step out, though I kept one tentative leg inside my room, my hand around the naughtiest doll's neck.

He held a mass of her beautiful old scarves, was rubbing them about his head, and chest and arms. He walked down the hallway like that, entered the den, did two or three turns about the room, stumbling, while pretending to be speaking to my mother—hiding his face behind all of that patterned silk, kissing at it, smelling at it, pulling it away from his face for a moment then starting again. He stumbled a second time and that second stumble is how I knew he was drunk, and though he drank every night this was the only time I saw him like that. *A drive. Through the woods*, he said. *Into the woods and after a few quiet hours we'll get to the pool there in the middle of that forest which is fed by a natural spring. Someone, no one knows who, keeps this pool stocked with thousands of gardenias. Floating on the surface of the water: And you swim and dip and float with them there, you and the flowers, you on your back with your eyes closed and the scent of those gardenias coming at you from all sides. And it is nicest at dusk or in very early morning, when there are few other people around, and the water is so cool and the air is hush silent.*

And when you come out of the water, Mara, you smell like the flowers and you keep this scent with you so that the memory of that pool soothes and calms you wherever you go the whole day through. I had never heard him speaking like this, soft, slow and poetic, though he was slurring and rubbed and rubbed at those scarves while he spoke, as if it were them he was addressing.

Papa. Papa. What are you doing? I called out, cautious, scared. He turned fast and saw me then, came right at me, rushed clumsily and tripped before trying to grab me, so that I turned abruptly away and dropped the doll with a thud, *Mama, Mama,* it moaned.

And he answered the doll as if it were me, *Yes, yes, your Mama, your Mama…*

I screamed shrilly, then, and began to cry.

My father realized where he was, woke up as out of a trance, flipped his head around and saw that he was crouched, here, in front of his weeping daughter, wrapped up in my mother's old scarves. And he cried, quiet, too then.

And pretty soon it was me, at eight years old, who was comforting him, patting his back and telling him to shush, shush, try to shush; Blinker running confused circles around us.

Angry daddy

He never spoke about her. About himself, about them. Not in a real and actual way. What I mean to say is that though he did talk of her, it was always dreamy, like a story, a fairytale or myth from out of one of my books. Never real. Nothing actual. Never about concrete things they had done together, places they had been. What she was like. What he had been like with her. Substitute scarves. This was about all he could manage.

It happened rarely, but he got angry too. And I know I was the one who pushed for it. Directly, clear, not in some unintentional sub-conscious pop-psych way. It was an obvious relief; I wanted him to pull out of his own head and see what I was doing even if only in anger. And he tried, punished me for smoking in our front room when I was thirteen, lighting up just as he was set to arrive. *Don't worry*, I urged Mineko in her little girl full-tulle skirt, lit match up to her face, *he doesn't care*. She glared at me, her long black hair flipping around behind her as she shot her head back toward me, astonished, while he walked right by us and into the kitchen when he finally did arrive. Even I was surprised at his lack of response, though I pretended nonchalance and kept right on smoking when her nervous giggles began. And later, when I walked into the kitchen long after she'd jumped on her bike—patent leather shoes and frilly socks pedaling hard—he said he'd be taking all cakes away from me for a week, though he did not look toward me as he said it. *Please don't*, I said near disgust. Had he really not noticed that I never ate his sweets?

I got caught ditching another time; I'd skipped nearly a month of school, had tried to make it obvious, though he did not see until he got that letter in the mail, from some school official I had never heard of. *No No No*, he moaned in protest, but he was not convincing. Was barely present even then, because there he stood in front of me, letter in hand, his face contorted with the frustration of having to do something now, forehead furrowed, eyes coming closer together; there he stood in what to other eyes might have looked like concern, yet all it took was one sharp comment from me; all it took was me looking back into his questioning eyes with pained determination: *How dare you?* I cried. *How dare you, pretend to care, how dare you hold someone else's letter about me in your hand like that? They have to tell you? Other people have to tell you to notice, tell you how to feel?* and my poor father's awkward anger crumpled into further disorder. *God! I don't even matter to you*, I screamed. And he stared back, baffled, not at all sure what he should do.

Perhaps I should be sorry now. I didn't know how to say things any other way, how to ask for what I needed, though I don't know that he would have been able to give it to me even if I'd known what I needed was. And so as a child all my dolls were beheaded, lacked limbs, were made to sit penance in scary dark corners. By twelve I was smoking, though I did not particularly like it. At fourteen I was watering down his alcohol to hide what I had drunk. The next year Mineko and I were selling her brother's Ritalin, a surprisingly measured form of speed, to a bunch of kids at our school who wouldn't exchange a word with us about anything else.

Father. If he ever did notice anything, make a comment, he was easily backed into a corner, bewildered. There was no back and forth. My poor dad. He was barely even there.

Bastard girl

My mother was a beautiful woman, as all young mothers looked back on by their grown children always are. Though other than this I can guarantee nothing, am not certain of anything, have no firm grasp. For, other than that one time in the kitchen, I never dared ask. I'd instead wait until they spilled from him, his largely fanciful pronouncements. And, even so, I can tell you that she was always a sad woman.

It seems important to make it clearly understood that my father never uttered this fact to me, for he never once mentioned an emotional state, yet I always knew it. My father called her perfect. "Your mother was the perfect woman, the perfect wife; she would have been the perfect mother" he would say. And even as a child, I could see right through this. Because if in his eyes she were perfect, I very early knew, then he had never dealt with the real woman that she was. My mother had never been allowed to be my mother, Mara, herself. This was my first clue into her sadness. And by reading through the words he said about her, and looking at her eyes in those few pictures, I became firm in the knowledge of the mother's dolor.

I could make things up for you, as I've grown accustomed to doing for myself. I could take the little he dropped and embellish for us both, you and me. I've done this for as long as I can remember, taken those bits he'd let fall and stretched them as far as they would go. I could certainly do it for us now, tell it in hushed tones so you understand the gravity, let you know that as a bastard girl she cried so many tears a river was formed in the valley between the hills which she called home; and that in their village, for my mother and father came from the same place, this river is still named after her, Rio Mara, in Central Mexico. I could tell you about her mother's rape, her mother's mother's rape, the rape of all the women of this town by the men who tamed land and each other with machetés and guns. I could tell you about how the weak were forced by the strong to work for a tortilla a month, a chili a day, a bean an hour. I could ask you to cry for the injustice of man, how he preys upon man and how man just sits back and watches and nods. I could tell you that she, being beautiful, was the only chance her mother had for an end of the suffering. Well, not for the end of the suffering, but for the end of the suffering in the manner in which it had presented itself thus far. The beauty of the daughter exchanged for the mercy of the man. They would move into his hacienda, his rancho, his home, have maids instead of be maids. But I think you have heard all of that before and I'm not sure which parts of it are true for her, and which parts I read in a dimestore novella.

I do know that when she met, and ran off with, my father, she was unhappily engaged to marry someone else. My father saved her. His one heroic act. And then the hero and his prize ran and ran dangling sugar cubes in front of the burro's nose so that the beast would pick up its pace. They ended up in this other world, across the border, where I now write you from.

I have heard that over there, across the river from where they swam, edging up to the border there in that other land, there are hundreds and thousands of wild donkeys and horses, all of them abandoned by their riders when it came time to cross to the other side. They roam the land together there, their heads stooped and working most of the time, pulling at and taking in and chewing the brush that grows up in tufts all around, their tails swatting at the

Mexican flies, the south of the border gnats. Once in a very long while these thousands of beasts simultaneously lift their heads to look after the memory—and for some it is only a genetic memory passed on from grandfather burros, grandmother horses—of a lost rider who left them there oh so many years in the past.

Anyway, this saving, this needing to be saved by my father, the most unheroic of heroes, is what I mean by my mother's sadness. This running away. This coming to live in a land without roots, with no mother, or good friends, or home. All of this is what I mean.

And then, as further proof, there are the three or four existing pictures. She is so young. And her eyes look directly at me; she never looks at my father who stands stiffly at her side, or at any other object within the boundary of the frame, but out and away, through the camera, as if only out there is there something for her, out to me. And there is nothing between us but this line of vision and I recognize a thing there in her eyes, which borders on tears, but is more like tears held in and which I know because I see it often in the mirror when I am all alone. I too am missing something, of course, and when I look into her eyes, this is, mainly, what I see.

If she were here, I would reach my hand out to her now.

And then again, her heart just stopped. Only very sad women die like that.

I forgot the detail of...

Did I mention that my father was a very big man? No? Well, my father was really quite fat. It fits in perfectly, you see. He was a baker, a candy maker. He'd had his very own bakery in Mexico long before the fact of me and then once here was hired to bake breads and cakes and such at a restaurant near our home but quit when I turned one. He liked it better this way, he said, his own big ovens, though now it makes a different kind of sense to me, his quitting just then. All the same, for as long as I can remember he worked at home, rising at four every morning, using the fruit in season for pies, whipping up perfect cloudlike meringues to be eaten individually as cookies are, making jellies out of guavas or tamarind, taking eggs right out from our chicken's bottom and transforming them into perfect flavor-laced flans, creating a whole alternate world out of chocolate and marzipan; his specialty was a cheese and grapefruit cake, the bitter tartness of the fruit stopping the sweetness from spreading too far into your mouth with every bite. At 8:00 he would wake me, and take me on his daily voyage, to deliver here and there, stores and restaurants and occasionally a private home for a party or such.

People would greet him with smiles, open arms, sometimes near tears for the occasion his treats so perfectly represented, for the thought of the coming melting of the sweet in the mouth at the ideally symbolic moment.

And then we would ride home together, me occasionally staring at the father, wondering at the pleasure he brought to so many others. Baffled by our own lack of happy occasions.

Once home he would spend the day mixing and testing, preparing for tomorrow's 4 AM. Reading out recipes and perfecting. Getting me to sample this one or that: "That was your mother's favorite," or if it were something new, "Mara would have liked this." Everything always inevitably through the taste buds of the mother. I'd secretly spit out whatever he fed me.

I never liked the father's sweets.

Deep dark

I want to take you with me, for warm protection and huddled whispers and conjoined musings; even if you resist a little, me pulling you along…

To get to the street beyond the back yard I have to climb down a steep incline. The earth moves under my feet, clumps of dirt and rocks roll down, crash and crumble on the sidewalk below. It isn't necessary to scramble in order to get there; I could have walked out the front door, half a block down and turned left onto the alley that leads to this other street. An easy walk. But I wanted to climb, and even as I slip down and scrape the side of my leg, I don't regret it. No blood and my bag fully intact, I wipe off the dirt, move toward the mouth of the trail which starts where this street dead ends, and step through the gate that marks that threshold. The ground is dry and hard, on either side the tall grass. And right after the first bend I am in the midst of a deep dark forest. That street at the back of my house, the one leading to this trail, is one I have walked thousands of times, though always in the other direction. I know it well. My cat lies in the middle of it sometimes, sunning himself, occasionally working furious at his fur, twisting insistent to lick at his own neck and chest from that prone position. But I have never seen the forest, even a hint of the forest, and now just thirty or so steps in and I am in the midst of it. My satchel is surprisingly light even with him in it, yet, although I have just started this trip, I am already tired; I begin to speak to my feet, to coaxingly remind them of how lovingly I painted their toenails, and still they do not want to go on. Perhaps it is this present tense that is wearing us out. For you were not, in fact, there with me, and it is exhausting to pretend; and so I must grant that it is over now and that we are looking back:

The woods were dark, as woods so often are. The light from the sky came down in little rays here and there and it was these that I decided to let guide me. I would walk from one diffuse ray to the next, firm in the belief that if light has represented knowledge for so many philosophers on so many deep voyages of the dark mind, then surely it could guide me in this voyage of my father's heart. I mouthed my brother's name, made it feel familiar on my tongue, tried once calling it out. I loved Manuel because I could shorten it to Manny or Manly or Man.

With his name on my lips I moved toward the next shaft of light and stopped short, my heart speeding. I stood statue still and, yes, I heard it again, the rustling up ahead. Instead of turning, hiding behind a tree, or running away in the other direction, I stood for one moment more and then I rushed toward it, reckless, and half believing I had already found him. I pushed through the low branches of an oak tree and saw them there in the distance, coming my way. I watched from my hidden spot as they approached, and after a short while a strange sense overcame me. I knew them, I felt. I worked hard to recall and it was only a few minutes before I placed them: It was the group from that day two and a half decades back. On that day, the woman who'd sold us our house had just walked in the back door; I'd stood for a moment of quiet reflection there with my dad, that group had appeared walking toward the path. My heart lifted now as I recalled it, *On an adventure*, my father had said, and here they were; it turned out he was right!

"Hello! Where have you been?" I called out. "It's been a long time! Are you hungry? You must be hungry.... Come and eat!" I rushed down yelling toward them. "Where have you been all this time? Where did you go? You came back! I'm off on an adventure now too! I have biscuits in my bag," I added, tripping, almost falling as I approached them, my hand already swimming in my satchel, hoping to entice. But they didn't look my way, not a glance, those four men and five women remained perfectly silent, their heads dropped, eyes focused down. Some wore robes in mustards and dark oranges and burnt reds; others were in loose tunics and pants in the same shades. The women all had long hair, gray now and flowing, mostly, though one wore hers up in a bun. The men were clean-shaven although three of the four had hair down to their shoulders or longer. They advanced in slow measured steps and were soon just before me, eyes still drawn down, grouped in twos and threes.

"I remember you," I said, low now, as they moved right by. Not even their skinny dogs were distracted, hadn't drawn closer, like any ordinary dog would, to check for safety, steal a sniff at my leg. Like strange medieval penitents trapped in the interior world of their remorse they'd all just passed me by, unhurried, in formation, and I was left standing, staring—silent too now—at their departing backs.

"But I need your help!" I called after them, not at all sure of what I meant. "I'm all alone!" And in the moment I yelled it I understood, at some deep level, that this was the point. Yet a part of me had to wonder, what was this place? And why did I feel compelled to be here?

It was hours before I could move from my spot. And then I walked, slow, in the direction they had come from. Their disturbingly familiar disregarding silence blanking me out even as it led me deeper into the pit of those dark woods.

Who likes sex?

Well if you don't you can skip this part.

I walked on and stopped at the side of a brook. I was shaken and thirsty and dipped my head in, my hair fanning out in the flow about me. I held my face down, under the water, which had seemed so beautiful, such a relief in the moment I saw it, and wondered what it would feel like to drown.

I pulled up sudden, dizzy and gasping, and fell onto the moss, pushed my dripping hair back, away from my eyes, brusquely wiped at my face; and as I wondered at the war that was being fought inside me I heard a crackling, turned, and saw sparks flying up as a log fell in a fire the penitents must have left behind. I approached the warmth and saw the remnants of a big sheep—head intact and lying bloody before me though the limbs had been cooked and torn apart—piled haphazardly near the flame. Those vegan-looking penitents were serious meat eaters it seemed. I sat myself down in front of the fire and relaxed into its heat but soon a loud banging interrupted, startling and nearly choking me as I chewed at a chunk of that roasted lamb; I swallowed quickly and focused scared in the direction of the commotion. And I saw my dog. There she was, walking out from behind a huge boulder to the left of me which I was only now seeing. "Blinker!" I yelled… and she ran toward me, rubbed her muzzle into my leg and my hand dropped down as if we'd been together just last night. "Hey, old girl," and my long dead dog gave me her paw for a moment before walking up to my head and licking the remaining water from around my face. I handed her a big bone to gnaw then, whispered and reminisced for a while, and with my arm around her neck we fell asleep.

With Blinker, now, full and fully satisfied. In sleep, toward the dawn of the new day. The night was cold but the fire was good and they later confessed that it was because of the warmth of this and the smell of cooked meat, not the pheromones at all, that they approached. There were twelve of them, and I will not go on with the analogy here because I don't want to be accused of a lack of religious piety. I tell it as it happened, and as it happens there were twelve. They were of the Nordic variety, Teutonic young men. And after they had sniffed about and eaten a good chunk of lamb they very patiently, and almost sweetly, let me sleep.

They waited for three days, they say. Though time in the woods is something hard to pin down and I've no way of knowing if they lied. And when I rose again, well, when I rose, they all wept. We didn't know if you would ever return to us, they said in unison.

I never knew I had been to you to begin with, I replied, as I sat up and wiped clumsy at my eyes.

They asked me to stand up and twirl around and then they asked if they could touch. No, I shrieked, and Blinker growled a long low growl as they approached with outstretched hands.

We just want to make sure that you are real, they said. I am, I answered indignant, and then I looked at Blinker and understood why there might be doubts. It was then that one of them, the smallest of that blond lot, said: I think this one is a Mexican. I see it in her eyes, the fullness of breast, the width of the hips, the brownness of skin.

Please, they all exclaimed in full and Nordic chorus, let us put our heads on your chest. Cook us food that makes us sweat; make it so hot that we hallucinate. And when I yelled at them and told them to shut up, to stop it all right there, the tallest one, the one with the long and flowing locks chuckled and elbowed at the others and said, "She's a spitfire alright." The rest nodded back, eleven smiling heads moving up and down, and when they grew tired of this gesture the most middle sized and average looking one spoke on: Sing to us in your sweet Mexican voice. The one with straight, shoulder-length hair and the biggest ever blue eyes added: Teach us how to dance. "Yes, yes, teach us how to dance!" they all yelled in unison, "How to dance!" even louder, and when I tried to run away, they drew up in a circle around me.

Of course I fainted. When I rose again, and this time I knew it was again, I was in a cave. They had apparently carried me up a cliff, taking turns at swinging me across their backs, passing me down the descending line of climbers, Blinker bringing up the rear. When they finally got me up there they laid me down in the center of the cave and when I woke they all wept. We didn't know if you would ever come back to us they said in unison. I'd heard all that before and know I wasn't looking very pleased.

"Listen," I said, "I'm sure you are all very nice young men, clean and well-bred, but I've got some things to take care of, have a brother to find, some things to set right, and I really can't hang out here in your cave."

They all nodded that familiar condescending nod and then the head guy, the one with the particularly flowy golden locks told me that they had some corn they wanted me to grind and turn into tortillas for them. There was a little pile of vegetables and chilies near a mortar and the rest of the lamb was spread out by the fire, "We got you everything you need. We want to have a Mexican feast tonight. We are going to have an Aztec party," he went on.

Well I know how those Aztec parties always end, a heart—still pumping—in someone's outstretched hand, so I started shaking and in a staccato stutter told them that they didn't understand … I didn't know what to do with all of this stuff … my father had always done all of the cooking. They had me all wrong; if there was any Indian in me at all it was most probably Totonac, not Aztec, no sir, my father's grandmother had been from Veracruz, after all. And besides, I said, I usually just do take-out; someone must surely deliver up here? And if not I'd like to get going, just have to grab up my things; and as I started walking toward the entrance of the cave Locks grabbed me by the arm and set me in front of the fire. "Cook," he said in the deepest and most authoritative tone I had ever heard.

"Yessir," I answered.

I got busy—moving things around, carefully placing cilantro or onions in this pile, then cocking my head and deciding they would look more aesthetically pleasing over there in that one—when out of the corner of my eye I saw them pull out the tequila. Well, I was taken violently aback and stopped all of my arranging, for it was a well known brand, that *Don* is probably what you have in your liquor cabinet at home.

"Hey!" I yelled; Locks turned and, shocked, looked at me mid-gulp. "Where did you get ahold of that?" I went on. "Why didn't you just buy your tortillas at the same market where you got that, or the restaurant around the corner? Why enslave me here in front of this rather large and fuming fire? I'd prefer to be drinking with you."

"Quiet," said Locks in his convincingly official voice. "For now you are the mother. There will be plenty of time for you to be the whore," he nodded sagely at the other eleven before going on, "Now, cook."

"Yessir," I answered.

It was, not surprisingly, a horrible meal. It is pathetic, really. You'd think that after over twenty years of ignoring my father I would have picked something up. I hadn't. When Locks started to complain at the lack of tortillas, I told them all that that was the way the Aztecs ate their maize, as a gruel, thick and lumpy. I said it in my most convincing voice and added some meaningful hand-gestures, nods and concerned looks. "If you want to have an Aztec feast, you will have to actually eat like Aztecs," I said, hands on hips now, making sure to look ashamed at their lack of knowledge and dedication. I think they only half believed me, but it didn't matter, as the twelve had drunk themselves silly and actually had very little idea of what it was that they were eating. Quite a bit of what they chewed fell out of their mouths anyway, and there was laughter and yelling and half-hearted punching and wrestling between them, all of it going on simultaneously.

They passed out halfway through the meal. It was a shame really, because that one, the one with the straight shoulder-length hair and cartoonishly big blue eyes had struck my fancy. Now, I've read books and I knew that they would take turns guarding the entrance to their cave when it came time for sleep. I had imagined waiting with one eye open until it was his turn to sit out there. Myself sneaking past the other sleeping eleven. Hans there, at the door. I would have to whisper to him. He would turn quickly, startled, body stiff. I would have to whisper again and shush him, "Where was your mother?" he would ask. "Shhhh," I'd whisper back and then I would bend down slowly and kiss at his neck. "You said your father always did all of the cooking; why no mention of your mom?" I would kiss him more deeply then and his body would relax, silent now, and give so that I could begin to bite at him a bit. A groan from deep within. At that I would gently slide my hands down his chest to his loins, let him touch at me, a bit too eagerly at first so that I would have to whisper to slow down, "Slow down," as I climbed up on top of him. And then I would see his big eyes close, the questions ceased now, as I moved my hips in rhythmic regularity.

It turned out that they all fell asleep drooling in front of the fire, their mouths spitting out occasional susurrations about tequila and Aztecs and a Mexican princess. Hans muttered something about a Chinese Goddess and I turned quickly back around to make sure he wasn't mocking me.

I picked up my father, woke up the dog and tip-toed out unnoticed. I wasn't forced to seduce Hans, to trade sex for freedom—like Judith with Holofernes—at all.

As it turns out

was not the first one.

Gauguin may have been a great painter but in the end what really fascinates us about him is that he liked to fuck the brown girls.

And this…

After the slow and sneaking tippy-toe got me past their entrance, I rushed through the woods at a noisily quick pace: whipping branches, crunching leaves, my own only partially withheld underthebreath curses. I was trying to gain as much distance between me and the boys as I could before daybreak. I firmly decided that for the remainder of the trip I would not be eating any more meat, and thus avoid attracting groups of marauding men. Berries, those biscuits I'd brought, nuts and the occasional fish would have to do.

I was rushing clumsy, running out of breath, when I tripped over my own feet and fell, lay there in a pile for a few painful moments and then flipped onto my back and stared up into dense branches, interwoven black outlines in the dark blue night; in my erratic snatches of breath I turned toward my dog where she'd landed beside me, and as I reached out to her for comfort, my fingers nearly to her head, she disappeared before my eyes. I gasped out in horror as I lost my dog for the second time in my life, my hand flying to my mouth. I lay still, staring straight for a long time, there on that one black spot.

It was after I drew myself up and began walking again, at a dis-
tressed and agitated pace, my chest heaving with the emotion, that
I came upon a beautiful, perfectly round and gigantic blueberry
bush, thorn free and surrounded by velvety moss. It stood there as
a gift to me. And though it seemed a cheap consolation, I wiped at
my eyes and took it in; then, exhausted, decided that I would sleep
under it for a while.

I gathered twigs and leaves for bedding, slowly piled and
methodically moved and arranged them, then lay myself down and
placed my father under my head for a pillow (a strange though
active literalization, perhaps, of the support I felt I never got from
him during his life). I turned, and barely awake any longer, my dad
under my head, I saw her pretty red shoes.

She had neatly placed them under the bush as one might do
under one's bed. She lay barefoot, her toenails painted a silvery
white, not a yard away. I crawled over to her on my knees, grateful
for her presence. Her black hair was long, beautiful, like Mineko's
had been, came down almost to her waist. It was thicker than mine,
and straighter too. I noticed she was wearing the exact same skirt
and sweater as me and my heart raced a little with the excitement.
We were as twins, and when I looked closer I noticed that, like
Mineko, she was Japanese. She was my Japanese twin! This is a very
good sign, I told myself. I was, after all, on the search for a twin.

And enveloped in the comfort of this thought I placed my
father back in my bag and then lay down close enough to her to
feel her body heat, an ease to the cold of these dark woods. I
whispered a nearly silent good-night, breathed in and out three
times, and fell asleep.

"I didn't know if you'd ever wake up," she said to me the next
morning. It sounded surprisingly familiar and I had to wonder why
everyone in these woods was so concerned with my sleep. "I found

these biscuits in your bag, and while you slept I had plenty of time to whip up some jam out of the blueberries. Here, have some," she tossed her long black hair behind her back.

"You look so much like an old friend of mine, that gesture, the way you toss your hair. Mineko."

"That's Japanese. I'm Chinese. My name's Lily. Very different cultures, you know." Her curtness was a shock.

"Yes, people always assume I'm Mexican."

"Where are you from?"

"I'm Mexican… my parents were Mexican. I guess I meant that they just assume it, that nobody even asks," I added awkwardly. "As if there are no differences," I went on, trying to express my sympathy with her position and expecting her to respond.

But she just stared for a few moments and then looked away as she nibbled at her biscuit. I picked one up and watched her as I ate.

It was only later, when we were together cleaning up, that she began to talk again and I found some things out about her: She was traveling through the woods looking for her father. He had left her, her mother, and two younger brothers five years ago. They needed him now as their mother was ill and could no longer work like before. He had a responsibility to the family which he needed to respect, they had all agreed, the two young boys nodding furiously as Lily stroked her sobbing mother's back. They had never allowed themselves anger at his vanishing before, had never discussed it at all, as if it were not a reality, *their reality*, as if his there one day gone the other were not something worth bringing up… but now they tossed their anger around like a heavy ball, each adding a cautious though wrath-wrapped phrase before dropping it and waiting for the next to pick it up and give it life, bounce it back into the air:

"He shoont have gone."

"How could he, just leave like that?"

"And us left behind."

"Our sadness."

"The hole in our lives."

"Where is he now?"

"He must come back."

"He has a wife."

"And sons need dads."

And me left behind, my sadness, where was she now, why had she gone? The hole in my life.

"Isn't the lack of a parent always deeply moving?" she asked.

I looked at her confused, my head spinning, wondering if she'd somehow heard my stray thoughts but as she continued her story I decided she'd been referring to herself, not me, for she immediately went on to tell how it was that her mother had sent her as messenger into the woods after her family's choppy discussion, in search of him. She said something about asking him to come home, the letter laying it all out.

Still worked up, I interrupted without really knowing what I was saying: "My father just died. I have him here in my bag." I looked away from her and at the bush as I heard what I'd just said, and hoped she hadn't been listening. "I'm here looking for my brother. His name is Manuel." That's as far as I went. It was none of her business, really.

"A brother," she said, shaking her head. "That isn't so important. Mothers and fathers, they are the ones."

"You're wrong, Lily," I insisted, a bit agitated now, for I only wanted to talk about Manuel. "A father and a brother can be the same thing. For a father is often a brother and a brother very often becomes a father. And sometimes, sometimes a brother can lead you to a father or a father to Manuel. Anyway, he's a twin. That's got to count for something."

"Still, siblings are expendable. One more or less is not going to kill anyone, but a parent..." she answered.

I was now really edgy, and growing increasingly upset with her, but some strange and unhinged part of me seemed to need her approval too; and so I forced myself to stay there even as my urge to flee was growing stronger.

"Let's just drop it, okay Lily. Comparisons don't help at all. Each is, and can only be, each. What have you done since you've been in the woods?"

It was then that she told me she'd had sex with Hans. They picked her up, the twelve, just as they'd done me. They carried her up to their cave, draped across their backs. They made her fix up a huge Chinese feast. She prepared sixteen courses: Dan Dan noodles and dumplings, sautéed watercress in oyster sauce, shark's fin soup and cold duck, sea cucumber with rice noodles, stir-fried chicken with black bean sauce, spiced pork, salted prawns and pickled cabbage. Unlike me, Lily was a good cook and she knew how to make it all. The banquet took four and a half hours, and she wore a red silk dress as she served them. They sipped whiskey out of rice bowls as they watched her work slowly around the room. And then after they ate they all passed out. All except Hans, whom they had already agreed would sit guard.

"Damnit," I said under my breath. I shot her a searing look as she continued.

"I was glad it was him," she went on, as if in a trance, "he was the best looking one. I waited until the rest of them were asleep and then I snuck past them. Hans was there at the door. I had to whisper to him. He turned quickly, startled, body stiff. I had to whisper again, shush him and kiss at his neck. I felt his body relax and give so I began to bite at him a bit. A groan from deep within. At this I gently slid my hands down his chest to his loins, let him touch at me, a bit too eagerly at first so that I had to whisper at him to slow down. I climbed on top of him and saw his big eyes close as I moved my hips in rhythmic regularity." She sighed.

"Alright already, enough," I huffed as I got to my feet and tied up my satchel, which she had very rudely left wide open.

"What's wrong?" she asked, eyes blinking quickly, startled, confused.

"I've got a brother to find, Lily. I can't sit around and listen to fairy tales all day long."

And with that I strutted off.

"You should stick your father in the ground where he belongs," I heard her call after me.

Must we always go back?

was exhausted, but felt the need to go further in, now, the depths of the forest. I wanted to crawl to a profound hidden spot, lie there alone. To find a patch of thick moss and nestle my head, shut closed tight my eyes, and float in the black.

I felt her cover me up, gently, then. "You okay?" her soft voice a thin wash.

"I'm fine," I replied.
"Take your time."
"I think I'm fine."

I see my brother, a boy, lying in bed, me there next to him, blanket held up to our little heads. I can just make us out, the same size, our faces close together and our sibling whispers texture the entire space, they make up the whole room, late into the dark mysterious night. There we are again, seven or eight this time, my hair falling long down my back, his a mess of tangles dipping into eyes; we're standing shoulder to shoulder, our clothes dirty, in a corner of the playground, wary of the big groups of other children and their obscure hierarchy-emblazoning pranks. Manuel and me, teenagers now, telling jokes with his friends, a joint passing freely between us, sexy sixteen, smashed and laughing behind our dilapidated garage. Babies again, three or four, our tiny hands, itsy fingers intertwined, our father looming up above us, a cart full of his baking goods in the grocery line. And there I am, seventeen, crying, screaming into Manuel's face, for being willing to learn how to bake with our dad. "You can't," I yell. "Don't you know what it means for you to be so willing to do that?"

"I'm not the angry one," he replies.

But none of this is real. Because instead of all this, instead of my brother, a twin, the closest of siblings, there is a blank.

My mother and father, two blanks.

My family: Blank. Blank. Blank. Scariest of all: the threat of myself becoming a blank.

What I do know about my mother and father is that there was nothing joint, nothing active. In my father's version my mother had just died.

Yet, to go forward we must always go back, they will tell you.

I don't know if I believe them.

Still, I feel the need to go on. Make stories to fill in the nothing. The sickening gap. In order to find Manuel, I've convinced myself, even if it's with tall tales, I have to fill in the blanks. So: I have told you that the father took my mother and ran off with her soon after they met. It is true that they came from the same place, the same town, and yet they had never met until shortly before the fleeing. There are many explanations for this, their not meeting, even though by any of our standards it was a small town. One of the explanations is this: My mother was as Elvis' Priscilla.

I've told you that she was promised to another man when they met. Well, she had been thus promised for six years when father first saw her. Since before she had turned ten. My grandmother, her mother, was given the right, the privilege, to live at his house, Don Refugio Basta's, and take care of her daughter, the intended girl, until she turned sixteen. My mother's mother could of course go on living with them after the wedding, though her role at that point would necessarily change. She would be more mother-in-law than mother from that day on. There would be different kinds of duties assigned to her. She would be the dame of the house. But she would no longer be permitted to sleep with the girl.

This all seemed a good life to my grandmother. The sacrifices seemed small in her book—the options seemed worse. They now had servants, would never again have to be servants. And he would protect them, in a way. Though the girl was kept almost always indoors, and was never, not ever, allowed to go out alone.

It is not that he could not have married my mother at thirteen or fourteen, or even younger, for Don Refugio made the laws in that place, but the girl was a crier, I have already mentioned that, and she cried and begged to be allowed to have her full childhood, until her fifteenth birthday, and then she was successful in begging for the entirety of the year after to be able to enjoy the memories of all that had gone before—of that childhood—before he took her as rightfully his. Then she could start clean. A cut with the past. She would keep her side of the bargain. But not until she was sixteen, until then she wanted to be a girl.

Tears did not usually bother Don Refugio. Tears were nothing to him. He had seen them, been the cause more often than not, on the thousands, millions, maybe billions of occasions when he had seen them. But this girl. This girl with her soft eyes, with those soft eyes all wet, it was not right. This girl who could make a river flow, could maybe make an ocean, and here in Central Mexico that was not right. This girl was a beauty. That many tears from her, no, it was not right. If they could keep her eyes just a little bit drier by giving her a few years, well, now that was alright. She was there in his home after all, guarded over by her mother and all the other servants, and if ever she was able to get out there were men and more men who would stop her. It was safe. And, besides, he liked having her wander his halls, his patios, the furtive glimpses he would get of her as she moved about in her daily activities. Her shadow on the walls, the crumbs she left on the table, her little footprints in the patio dust.

Of course he had peepholes drilled into the girl's and her mother's room, into their bathroom. He could inspect every evening as the mother brushed the daughter's hair, one hundred strokes with a silver handled brush. Could see the girl as she pulled dresses on and off, nightgowns on and off, slips and other underthings up and down. He could observe while the mother scrubbed at the girl's back with a thick loofah as the child sat forward in the tub. Could watch the daughter do the same for Mother, could study them as they changed positions and then see the girl's little hands barely able to work that big wet loofah up and down her mother's back. Could look as they powdered and perfumed each other's bodies, scrutinize as they rubbed emollient oils into those stubborn parts, elbows and knees, thighs and feet. Could dream about all of their ablutions in that half-awake sleep before the real depth comes.

He didn't mind that the young Mara would turn her head when she saw him, walk with the front of her body facing the wall when he was in the room. Her fear did not bother him. It added something further to her charm, her tender apprehension. It added something to his dreams of her, her coy and tender apprehension. The fact that he had told himself that he would not touch her until she was sixteen, well, the anticipation of it made it somehow better; the excitement of that day was what he imagined when he raped his workers' wives. He was a man who could have anything he wanted, and to have this one thing on which there was a constraint, hmmmm, it made his blood boil. It made him scream when he pierced his workers' daughters.

He was a Catholic. He knew how to ritualize the passions, how to symbolize the act.

Little Mara, wispy in her white dresses, tears in her eyes, grass and leaves in her hair from all the time she spent laying on the ground in the patio, looking at the sky, the only way out. Out in the enclosed patio of the walled in home was only up and out.

Out was the sky.

All middles
have beginnings

She was at the market with her mother. As my grandmother nobly stood discriminately sampling dainty nibbles of fruit from the merchant's knife, Mara in her white dress crossed over and stepped up to my father's little stall to buy a candy mouse. A tiny chocolate mouse with eyes of pink marzipan.

My father's own eyes fell upon her, were instantly glued there; he knew sweets, recognized sugar, sucrose, fructose, honey, glucose, and molasses when they took a human form. And his eyes were frozen. His hands shook violently as he reached for the tiny treat she pointed at, his voice stttuuuuttterrred as he asked: this one? His legs grew wobbly so that he almost fell as he reached forward to hand it to her. Time stopped as her little hand reached out to take it, and then it went backwards so that my father was actually in the womb when her diminutive fingers brushed against his palm. Then, as he watched her walk off, my father's heart ran in his chest, leapt out of his mouth, and did two turns about the Zocalo.

She hadn't noticed him at all, and very simply skipped to seize her mother's hand.

Some beginnings develop middles

The mouse must have impressed her because from then on, twice a week, while her mother stepped between the nasal shouts of the calling vendors, from piles of fruit to mounds of vegetables, spices, cheeses, fishes, and meatses, the adolescent Mara visited his stall. My father's body would reverberate at each of her tiny steps toward him; he would work to pull himself together, to contain all of his excitement which only showed as a mild shaking by the time she finally reached his stall.

Sometimes it was a chocolate covered marshmallow, in the shape of a man—which she did not even notice was a wee edible sculpture of himself. Sometimes a cookie with cream filling, or a tiny single-person cake or tart. An Elephant Ear, palmier, made of layers of paper-thin dough. She always bought just one petite treat which she nibbled, holding her mother's hand as this woman royally haggled.

My father practiced at and successfully learned to control himself. Didn't shake so visibly in her presence. He still had a hard time looking directly at her as she decided on her sweet, but this he also worked at, turning his face toward her another fraction of an inch upon each subsequent visit. And then, after several months of these visits—which he had come to anticipate for days before, so that it was almost as if at the moment in which she stepped away from his stall my father was already waiting for the next Tuesday or Friday, mentally inventing an ever more enticing confection to place in his case for her discovery upon her return—he began to talk to her.

His speeches started with two simple and rather obvious, though lovingly spoken, words: "This one?" But rather quickly for such a timid young man of nineteen, he had moved on to other questions, had asked her her name, offered his own. And within a few more months they had an actual conversation in which, in the just over five minutes she gave him, and which he received as a most treasured gift, she opened up in the most miraculous of ways. It sprung out of her, her outlined story, as from a well which does not need much pumping. She had been holding it in for so long, had no one to talk to but herself and the sky, so that when these ears on the head of this young man were tilted toward her it all came out—the dirt-floored poverty in which she had lived alone with her mother, those happiest days of her life—then the discovery of her existence by Don Refugio Basta. She was just outside her and her mother's small shack, crouched and patient, trying to lure a feral kitten to her with a long string on the end of which she had tied a little piece of white cheese. She tossed it out to him and the kitten sprang back in playful shock and then hopped sideways at the cheese that the girl was pulling gently toward her. But instead of luring the kitten in, she lured the great big rat, Don Refugio, who just happened to be riding by. He focused on the girl, jumped off of his horse, kicked the cat aside, picked up the dirty piece of cheese, plopped it in his mouth, chewed, swallowed, and then followed the string to the dainty hand which was attached to the most beautiful girl he'd ever seen. By the time he got inside the door to meet the mother, he had decided that that girl was his.

Mara went on to describe her time in his house, his leering looks, his drooling grins, the sensation that she was always, always, being watched, being primed, fattened (Metaphorically speaking, of course, for she knew she was thin, maybe even too thin. She smiled to lessen the tension, before becoming all too serious once again.) for the sacrifice; she told of her tears—the little puddles she left at the table or out there in that enclosed patio yard—her coming nuptials. She sighed a deep sigh. In just three months and five days she would be sixteen, and then the month after: a wedding, her wedding, would take place.

Father stood, staring, overwhelmed by what he heard, breathing in and out so hard that her sweet hair moved lightly in the breeze that he created with his infuriated breath. He was not aware of the effect he was having upon her long brown tresses for in those seven minutes as confessor he did not even see her there, standing in front of him, and imaged her instead, in that grotesque man's home, being followed and watched, being leered at and drooled over. He could see her walking in halting steps down and toward the altar, holding the hand of the mother who would offer her daughter up thus, to that large and looming Basta. And when she turned to walk away, after this short confession, it was not Mara who had tears in her eyes, but my father.

He quickly turned his face away from his wares, afraid that the legion of tears now pouring out of him would melt and wash his sugary treats down the sides of his little counter and away into the dirty corridors of the clangorous market.

The plan

My father is a mere boy, a young man full of yearning, and heartache, and a desire to do right. He holds the pillow over his face and cries and cries, muffled moans pouring out from deep inside. He carries the weight of his own past indiscriminately mixed in with his love of sweet Mara there in his eyes. He lowers the pillow to his mouth and bites at the edge of it and you can see their swollen redness, their agony sag. His longing for the girl has become confused with what he calls his pity, his empathy for what she suffers. He imagines himself protecting her—sees himself in front of her little shack, positioning himself between that Basta and the beautiful young Mara. He imagines himself, larger than life, coming from out of nowhere to stand in front of and demand of Basta to go—get back on his horse and go—in the direction of his pointing finger. And don't even look back. Leave this girl alone forever. He imagines her gratitude, his awkwardness at his heroism—he looks down and kicks some stones and dirt around and tells her it is nothing, really. Then he feels her tenderness for him washing out toward him in thick waves; she moves in close and her lips slowly come near and then brush against his. He sees and then feels her arms wrapping around him, himself pushing into her body, laying his own arms upon, then around her, and finally leading little Mara down, into a prone position.

No.

He must stop.

He could not go any further. He punched at his groin—too scared, too awkward and timid to allow himself even the fantasy.

So instead he lay in bed that night, in the once—before the disgrace of his father's drunkenness—beautiful ancestral bed which stood dethroned and disgraced, rusting in the room next to the room his father slept in. He did not so much lie, actually, as toss and turn and sigh and cry before settling for moments at a time only to start the cycle again. She'd just wanted a little baby kitten. Something she could hug and squeeze and love. And instead she'd gotten a big cheese-eating rat. He knew Basta. He'd seen Basta. Everyone knew, everyone'd seen Basta. The man was a brute. How had he never heard that he was hiding this beautiful girl? The sweet, gentle Mara. How had he not known that an angel was being held hostage by that demon? Okay, that sentence was dumb, puerile even, nevertheless he cried and tugged at the collar of his t-shirt, tossed his legs over the side of the bed and got up and did two, then three, then fifteen turns about the room. He walked down the hall, into that other dank room and stared at his father who slept there, completely drunk and unaware of others' suffering. He sighed in bursting disgust and then he went back to his own room and got down on his bare knees and dropped his forehead firmly to the tile floor and begged for the strength to do something, to come up with something, to help that poor girl.

He awoke the next morning to one of his father's deep throated gurgling snores in that position. Bent forward in his underwear and t-shirt. On his knees and with his forehead imprinted with the flatness of the hard cold floor.

Will they give you a party? he asked her the very next time he saw Mara. For your sixteenth birthday?

Oh yes, she answered. Her mother had been planning with Don Refugio for quite a long time. This day, the man had expounded, could not go uncelebrated. It represented the end of his wait.

He was a Catholic. Let's remember that he understood the importance of rituals. A big, big party. And then a month later—for he didn't want to confuse dates in her mind, in her future a birthday would be one thing and an anniversary another—they would be married. That would be an even bigger party. And her mother had told her that she would have to hide her fear, put on a face of joy and celebration—smile and greet and eat and dance—at both these feasts.

Well, Mara, listen to me, he said. You must convince them that you love my treats. You must beg them to hire me to bake your cake, to make the candies for the celebration, to prepare the meat pies. Listen to me Mara, it is not the work that I am looking for; do you begin to understand me? It is not the fee for the work that I want—it is your freedom.

And then he told her that he loved her.

It was then that she looked at him. Then that she first lifted her soft hazel eyes (almond shaped, of course) and focused on my father, saw the boy, the young man, for what he was. Father was not yet what he became; if the surviving photographs can be trusted, I can say that he had a nice and gentle face in those days, and besides, he was already resolutely hers; of course she must have seen this, the way it was inscribed on his every feature. This young man was hers. He was all hers. His eyes stared at her and they matched the softness of her own; his full, dark red lips smiled limply up at her.

She immediately trusted him. She looked long and deep into those eyes, no small feat for little unsocialized Mara. Okay, she said. And then, in a very animated tone, she added that she would cry her first ever fake tears in order to get her way.

She touched his hand for just one second before she ran off that day.

"Mara!" he called out to her as she bounded away. But she was gone to him, already out of earshot, so he whispered it to himself, "Mara, you forgot your tiny treat," and then he lifted it to his own two lips, the guava and cream cheese cookie that he had made in the shape of a cherub.

He told her his plan at her subsequent visit: He knew of a plant, a fungus—all the best bakers know such things—which could induce sleep in the most stubbornly awake of wakeful men. It grows on the roots of the… and here he stopped himself—for all the best bakers know to keep these things they know top secret. It didn't matter where it grew, he added. What mattered was that he would mix this plant into everything he made. She must mind not to eat anything he produced for her party. No matter how good it looked, and it would look good, he added in an uncharacteristic show of shining pride. Then he grew serious and his voice softened a bit as he added that there would be time enough for her to eat his treats after they accomplished their mission. He smiled tenderly at her as he said this, paused a meaningful pause, but she continued to stare straight, wringing her hands and intent on hearing the details of his scheme so that he was forced to continue: She must also make it her task to ensure that everybody, every single one, eat several bites of at least one of his pastries.

You must promise me, Mara, and here Father leaned into her, had his face closer than he had ever had before, so close he took in the fullness of her scent through flaring nostrils. This one thing will be up to you, he went on—fairly swooning from her smell. Push the meat pies on anyone who tells you they don't eat sweets, he slurred.

Yes, she said, very matter of factly. Mother and Don Refugio were already almost convinced, she added nodding, would, in fact, be ordering some sample comfits from him the next week.

Le fête

We have been to parties like this. We know the long dresses, some so long that they dragged in slow trains behind the girls, las chicas, the dames. I turn and say that I would like to finger the smooth slick surface of all that silk, the slightly crisp crunch of the taffeta, the minute imperfections of the uneven, though exquisitely fine grain of the handmade lace. You want to step inside so you can hear the bustling skirts, you say, as you look at pinched up bodices. Want to stare openly at overflowing breasts, heaving chests, to touch and feel that flesh, the supple give. We look away from them and toward each other for just one moment before we again focus on all those sparkling lights and then we together walk in, into the glow of the many twinkling chandeliers and innumerable candelabra in that large, mirrored, baroque hall. You take my hand and before I lean in to kiss your beautiful cheek we both pause and with heads held together for one minute listen to the many musicians—groups of Mariachis strolling about with their huge, medium sized and tiny guitars, serenading this girl, then that—the shyest of that female bunch turning blushing faces from the deep bass of those songs, the more bold looking directly into the crooner's eyes, daring *him*, the working class musician, to match *her* stare, the elite and invited señorita, who, by the way, has Spanish or French blood coursing through her veins; and then the string quartets too. There must be something of everything here at this most important of all birthday balls, Don Refugio had said.

There were tables upon tables of laughing youths—open faces, shimmering eyes, gaping mouths—gathered together from all of the surrounding towns, none of them her friends but all asked to look as if they were.

The suits the men wore were mostly black, but here and there a man who feared not for his machoness had the daring to don a pastel colored one which he rounded off with snakeskin boots. All mustaches were perfectly combed, every strand of male hair was slickly greased back, though some allowed a slickened strand to fall casually onto the forehead or down near the left eye. The jewels the women wore glinted and shone, a hand raised coyly to a laughing mouth sending off millions of little rays of bounding, bouncing light which landed here on a glass of champagne, there on a young girl's long and curly tress. Their own hair, their womanly hair, was done up in clustered piles of stiffened curls which sat like crowns on rounded heads, so as to show off those bejeweled and gleaming necks and ears; and every time that the girls and boys and men thought that they'd never seen a head done up in such complexity all they had to do was glance to the left, glance to the right, to see that the next head of orchestrated curls rose up to a higher pitch than the last.

And the air, all of it, sat thick with the smell of food—baked and fried and grilled and sautéed—and perfume and intermingling snakes of smoke, and the waves of the music and voices singing whispering talking shrieking laughing. Reflected and refracted millions of times in those mirrored walls could be seen these tables upon tables of men and boys and women and girls reaching toward each other, caressing underfoot, stretching toward this or that course, daintily pushing food around plates as heads swung to look for *him*, to look for *her*. And everywhere the sight of dancing and chasing, of girl leading girl to look at young men, of young men standing back and smoking while glaring down cinched eyes at giggly femmes.

You have seen them, the little tiny boys and girls in poufy dresses and small tuxedoes, forced into each other's arms for the enjoyment of the adults, for the pleasure of laughing grown-up eyes asked to dance together. Of course there was one young boy, his eyelashes long and his cheeks red, who loved the attention so much that he started bringing the little girls out on his own, even when they pulled back in shy resistance.

And Mara there, at the head table, nervously biting her nails, twisting at the skirt of her dress, scratching at arms and legs. Looking up to nod at this or that person whom she'd never seen before.

How will I do it? she asks herself. How can I keep track of all of them? She wipes her smooth brow with her little pink kerchief, mops up the first sweat she has ever produced, and we think how lovely, how lovely she is, even in her nervousness. How sweet the sweat upon her kerchief.

We are rooting for her. We concentrate all of our power upon her.

And it was then that it came to her. It took a coming together of everything she had in her but two hours after the dinner had been picked up, in the middle of the dancing and drinking and smoking, she clicked at her glass with her fork: "Please, I have something to say…." it was barely above a whisper but then a bit louder she added: "Please."

Don Refugio looked her way and then ordered everyone to silence, standing straight and with severe gaze for the minute it took to calm the whole of that baroque hall.

And Mara cleared her throat and calmed her nervousness as best she could: I would like to make a toast to childhood, she said. Then a bit louder she added: To the end of my childhood. I would like to end it with a toast.

The excitement at her own cleverness sent her confidence soaring—which in turn sent her voice booming: And since it is a childhood toast, everyone must pick up a sweet.

They all sat quiet, looked about with confused eyes, some even daring to roll them at each other, but Don Refugio coughed a clearing of the throat, pulled himself even straighter still, and then nodded at the congregation in order to end that awkward pause. They dared to dart looks at each other for just one second before their reservations forcefully dropped; and then there was an immediate rustling which lasted for two or five minutes while the waiters passed the trays to and fro and to and eager hands reached and crossed and bumped each other as they grabbed for this and then that, cake and cookies and sweets.

Mara asked to have all the men who had gathered themselves outside brought in. And then, when they were all in her presence, she lifted her voice again: "Everyone," she said stiffly, and then to soften the effect of her "everyone" she gave a small laugh. They all joined in. Then little Mara picked her tiny treat up, and blew it a kiss, which made them all laugh even louder before they mimicked it, blowing kisses all around the room.

Don Refugio ran his arm through hers and then nodded at them all to bite down. They all chewed, the waiters, and the cooks too, and laughed and chewed, while Mara held her tiny candy mouse up in the air.

By the time she brought it down to her mouth, to pretend at a nibble, their eyes were all growing heavy, lids drooping, heads knocking. By the count of ten, they were all asleep.

What I know

t was velvet dark and vastly lonely in those woods. I turned my head to the side and blinked fully open my eyes, tried to remember how long it had been since I'd lain myself down on this moss. How long since I'd left those twelve men, Hans, my dog; and Lily, I thought about how I'd left her as well. Jealous and angry I had run off in a huff and now I had no one. And this led me to think about how often I let my uglier emotions take control of my actions, jealousy and anger and fear, as strong as independent beings, sometimes.

I pressed my head down into the moss, overwhelmed by this thought, my own hideousness, and, for the first time since I'd begun my trip, I began to shake with cold and uncertainty. I wrapped my arms tight around my frame and closed my eyes again; and I saw myself there, hanging on the backs of my eyelids, anarchic and clever, perhaps, but also smart-mouthed, and pissed and defensive. And then I scrunched my already closed eyes to erase, and saw her appear there, another me, well dressed, no dust and cat fur clumped onto her knee-length black skirt, no nails bitten down to nubs, no hair in messy disregard. She looked self-assured and well tended. And when she spoke, a line of tender sympathetic worry played upon her brow: "Why is it that you are always so ready for the attack?" she asked. "Why do you see the world as one big daunting venture in which you have to run away from this and that one? Why is your reality so full of failed relations and bitchy twins in competition, and incompetent fathers and dead from sadness mothers? Why do you think you have to fuck for freedom and walk off in a huff and carry on my father's legacy of daily killing my mother in your vast unacknowledged anger at her vanishing?"

"I don't know," the dirty me replied.

And then I scrunched my eyes again and they were both gone. I was gone, just a vapor, now, once again floating on the moss.

I returned to my body only as my ears began registering the shrieking bird calls, the wild animal roars, all of those beings around me which were making their presence clearly known but who refused to show their forms. Things *moved* in the forest, I knew. And the lack of form, the hearing but not seeing, caused my fear and uncertainty to sink yet further in.

And to match the velvet pitch outside, and the depth of my dark sentiments, I still carried, inside of me, this black familial void. This shadowy nearly nothing which made me so uncomfortable that I'd begun to make up stories, to attempt to cast light through my own invention: Father—not a hero, Mother—young and scared and such a beauty. Why had they run off? And, just as puzzling, why did it seem so important for me to try and make it all fit? Did I really believe all that stuff about knowing yourself: that to begin to face the mystery of me I had to know them?

Because if I was going to subscribe to that, I had a big problem here. There was an awful lot of invention in my version. How could I justify filling up the holes and fissures and gaps with so much that was made up? Was this any way to get at the source of things? And in the end, after all that work, what if the gap was all there was, no source at all, only that space that I'd been working so hard to fill in with words and more words but which like a dragon in some fairy tale was never quite full.

I heard the dragon roar, saw the licking tongue of fire darting out in its approach.

"Manny!" I yelled out on the fifth night. I couldn't go on lying there, I suddenly decided, trying to figure them out without going on myself. I had to move. They were both dead, and for me to work so hard to try and figure out all their reasons why suddenly seemed a big mistake. I began shaking again, broke into a sweat, felt around my head with unsure fingers and came away with tips all wet.

Besides, what if I got so stuck in their reasons that I failed to go on myself? What if you could get stuck in the going back? The terror of what you find in that backward glance big enough to paralyze. Turn to salt. I had heard of that happening. Sick in the heads that never leave their beds. What if I became one of them? Freud's Wolfman. Little Hans. What if I never moved again?

It was then that I gathered together everything I had in me and pushed and pulled myself up from my cold mossy crib. Better to move blind than get stuck so I stumbled, and fell. I pushed up again, reached out for a nearby tree trunk and took my first in five days stiff steps: "Manny! Man!"

"What are you yelling at?" a flat low voice behind me asked, hot breath falling moist onto my back.

I raised my head, startled, a chill running through my spine. My body tensed. And then, in the moment before turning a strange sense of relief overtook me, for I was not alone. I did turn then and saw him there before me. He was large, a very big man. His skin looked dry and dead as if no blood coursed beneath in an olive shade that verged on green. Clearly, he saw no sun. His hair sat on his head like a thatch and he almost completely lacked lips, as if his mouth were just a line that smiled or frowned or opened to expose his insides. He blinked his big protruding fish eyes, brown, repeatedly, like a nervous twitch, while I took him all in. Despite those rapidly blinking eyes he seemed almost serene—or was it cold composure?—as he stared back at me.

I gazed with circumspection and when my eyes had done their rounds he reached up toward his mouth with one long sinewy finger: "Shhhhh," he insisted sharply. "There are many people here in these dark woods who are trying hard to get some sleep."

"You're enormous, a giant," I uttered slow with awe.

"Well, technically at 7 foot 4 I miss by two inches. So I'm actually just a big guy." He seemed proud in his response and pulled at his frayed suspenders a bit. "Now, what about you? Isn't sleep what you came for too, Ramona? Or have you got other big plans?"

"How do you know my…"

"Now, really. Must we? You don't expect me to play along with all that do you? There's a lot that we could talk about, Mona, if in fact you don't want sleep. But first let's leave the stupid questions behind, shall we? There is so much to discuss in the here and now. For instance, what are you doing here, now?"

"I don't know."

"Come now. Don't be so boring. You've been a nasty little bitch most of your life and now you're here and you don't know why that is? You're just like your mother, who also liked to pretend she didn't know how she got to the places she did."

"How dare you? What do *you* know about my mother?"

"No need to be so testy. I don't know much. But I'm sure you're about to fill me all in."

"Well…" I began, further unnerved, for I somehow felt that the line between us was slipping and what was being lost was my sense of determination, "sometimes I do feel as if I knew her. Know her, still know her. I'm certain there's a lot I've gotten from her. I'm miserable most of the time. I know that. I'm unsure of what I want, that's true too, but feel that I wouldn't know how to get it if I did know what I wanted was. My inability would just serve to frustrate and make me insane and so it's just as well that I don't. But sometimes I can see her. Not like in the pictures, static, rather moving around, doing things. Talking to people. Or avoiding their eyes so she doesn't have to say hello. Loving people. Or getting angry at, or with, or because of, them. Shopping. Eating. Preparing for bed. She's shy, I think, quiet, maybe. She often uses too much salt in her cooking and likes to drink white wine. She dyes her hair red, sometimes, blonde. She bruises easily and gets lost alot. She doesn't like to drive. But I try not to think about these things. About her. Or about me. Or about her and me. Or about her without me. Or me without her. I try not to think."

"But you can't help yourself can you? You know she made a choice don't you? You *have* thought about that. She weighed her options, didn't she? Father and daughter in one hand, a new fuck and her son in the other. Hmmm. We both know what she chose. Ancient history, no?"

I stared at his mouth, that sick line, and commanded my legs to run. But they refused me, collapsed worthless under my weight and I fell in a shattered pile on the spot where a moment before I had stood.

He came over to me then, sure of himself, smug. He took his big heavy hand and raised it to a clumsy caress at my head there where I'd fallen and then he repeated this action over and over again. I wanted to push him forcefully away, defend myself with violence, but I didn't have the strength. "It's okay," he said, softening to convince, "I'm here now." His voice went to a whisper, "I know you like me, Mona. I can see it. I know you do. And I like you too. You're so lovely. Close your eyes. Shhhh. Go on now, darling. Sleep."

His voice chilled me but my eyes did close then, against my will. And then I felt his big and callused fingers rub upon my chest. I raised my eyelids, though they were lead, and saw that his eyes had fallen slightly shut and a languorous smile had begun to play about his mouth. Spittle was gathering at the sides of this lazy smile and his tongue was lightly licking. I focused on and saw those waxen outstretched fingers as they moved in rough untidy semi-circles up my thighs. I saw the dirt, encased under the nails, thick black arcs like heavy frowns. It was this small detail that fully woke me, somehow gave me strength.

"What do you think you're doing?" I shrieked as I bolted up from my recline.

"Come on, Mona. I'm here for you. Sweetie. Darling. But you must be for me too. I did ask you. I asked you if you liked me... I don't *always* do that," and here he dropped his big face down and close to mine, his hot and thick stench breath blanketing me so that I broke out in an immediate sweat.

"But I didn't answer... I never said that you could..." I gasped disturbingly uncertain.

He took his still outstretched index finger then and brusquely rubbed insistent on my breast.

It was someone else's mouth, not mine at all. Her head bent into that frowning finger and it bit down upon it. Hard, teeth gnashing to reach at bone. And when he scrambled up to his feet, screaming and shaking me free of him, I ran.

"Mona!" I heard him yell. "Come back here!" Authoritative deep and long into the woods. "I command you to come back for the night!"

My cement heavy legs did move for me this time. And though in my half-dream escape I seemed to barely progress—my feet rising and dropping in what felt like slow motion as the cheap cartoon background repeated itself so that I seemed to be running past the same set of trees again and again—I ran. I ran.

Fine time for nothing

ran and I came to the end of the forest. In case you were wondering, there is an end to the forest. I've seen it. There's nothing there. It's a blank page. The still surface of an interminable lake or a mirror with no reflection. And on the edge of this nothing there was a sign: Home: 2,000,0000 miles or two years. Woods: 3 steps or right now. I could either go through the nothing, wander through that without direction—for in nothing there is no up or down—for two years, or I could go back into the woods and look for my brother.

I thought it best to roam the edge a while before deciding.

I saw the log cabins first, there in the clearing that is the edge between nothing and the deep woods. Little log cabins and I realized that it was probably their very presence that explained that slight clearing. They were small. Seven or eight or nine all clustered together. I saw piles of leaves and kindling, some beautifully carved wooden toys lying about outside of them. I saw clotheslines strung between tree trunks. I saw raggedy but elaborate clothing hanging limply in the lack of air there on the lines. And then I saw the small dogs and goats. A chicken, and a rabbit or two. I walked toward these animals and whispered "Manny" and then a bit louder called out "yoo-hoo."

I kept inching, crouched and careful, to the back of the third cabin there in that semi-circle and it was then that I saw them, four children of various sizes, strangely dressed and none more than ten years old, all stooped and digging in the dirt. I straightened myself and walked up toward them, their dirty hands and knees; and when they saw me they all noiselessly scampered off behind the trees. I turned toward the hole they had been digging and saw that it was an anthill, their four sticks laying where they had dropped them haphazardly now surrounded by the ants which had turned on the sticks of their torture with the furor of panic beginning to recede, panic turned into attack. I sat a little ways off from these ants and looked around to see if I could catch sight of the children, but they stayed hidden there behind their trees. I knew they would be watching so I pulled my satchel into my lap and opened it, hoping that my tinkering about would bring them forth to me. I saw it then, there, the jar of blueberry jam which Lily had placed into my sack and I was saddened by this small gesture of kindness, embarrassed, again, by my own childish jealousy and the way it had come between me and one who could have been a companion. I pulled it out and caressed it, felt its weight and coolness there in my cradled hands; and when I looked up I saw their little faces, four, looking down at me in a line of wide eyes and curiosity.

"Jam," I said and then they crouched down and squatted around me and I twisted the lid open in a slow and articulated gesture, a performance for them to see. They all wore clothing much too large for them, adult sized, rolled up at the sleeves, skirts dragging on the ground, and like the clothes I'd seen on the lines hung between tree trunks what they wore looked as if it had once been glorious—elaborate fabrics and gold threading—though now it was dirty and tattered. I held the jar up to them without the lid and the tallest of those four, a girl, reached her fingers out to it and touched the surface cautiously.

"Here," I said, "like this." And I stuck my fingers in it and then slowly moved them to my mouth where I sucked at the sweet jam. The only boy, a bit smaller than the girl, stuck his fingers in and then licked at them a bit before holding his hand out to this biggest girl who licked and then laughed. Within seconds the other two girls had descended on that little upheld hand and the boy pulled it back with a shriek.

"No," I said. "There's enough for everyone." And before I knew it their hands were dipping and rubbing into the jam, and then they were plunging into the jar so that it became hard for me to hold onto it. I placed it on the ground and they grabbed at it in turns taking the jam and rubbing it on their hands and mouths, licking and slurping and then when there was nothing left in the jar the boy smashed it on the ground. They were going for the pieces of glass when I yelled at them: "No! That's bad. You'll cut yourselves."

They didn't like that. My yelling. Four angry heads turned slowly, eight slit and critical eyes thrust their wrath at me; and in those seconds of angry stares I examined their faces smeared in blue: all the straight noses and long-lashed eyes, high cheekbones and messy dark hair. "You'll cut yourselves," I repeated in a near whisper: "You'll hurt yourselves."

"No. We won't hurt ourselves." The tall girl enunciated every syllable through blueberry lips as she stared straight at me. But they ignored the glass anyway and walked back over. "What's in there," asked the big girl, sticky fingers pointing at my satchel.

"Yeah, what's in there," seconded the smallest girl, who had short curly black hair and green eyes, as she fell into my lap.

"You can look," I said. And then I held it open for them.

The boy reached in front of the little girl and plunged in first. He pulled out a biscuit which didn't interest him; he threw it like a ball against a tree and then laughed much longer and harder than that small action deserved, doubled over with arms wrapped around his sides. The older girl pushed him dismissively away and swished her hands around inside. "There's nothing good in there," she uttered near disgust.

I thought of my father then and was ready to grab my satchel back and squeeze it shut when the little one spoke up, "Let me see," she said, writhing around and holding her arms up from where she had landed, down by my feet. I passed it down to her and she stuck her head into the bag and pulled out the nail polish. She held the bottle up to the older girl who read it: "deep water blue." And when her sister (I had decided this fact) had finished reading, demanded, "I want some."

"Me too!" shouted the other three, and they became a bouncing, screaming mass.

So I painted their nails. The big girl first. Then the boy. The littlest girl. And they were all quiet and serious as I did this, waiting patiently for their turn and then concentrating while I painted, watching the slow working of the tiny brush. They then puffed their cheeks and blew and blew at their fingers and toes like I showed them, their finger and toenails now matching the smeared blue of their faces. Finally I got to the very quiet and really quite shy middle-sized girl. This one smiled up at me as I worked. "Do you like it?" I asked softly.

"Yes. It's very pretty," she whispered.

"What's your name?" I asked.

"Mona."

I stared at her for a minute. "Mona? That's my name too, you know." And she smiled up at me once again.

What's in a name?

Mona. Manuel. That was the boy's name and when I showed my excitement and then said really? I think I have a brother named Manuel, are you and Mona brother and sister, he said: I don't know.

He was digging in the mud, making a little moat to surround a castle he had built out of this packed mud and little pebbles, so I picked up a stick and dug along with him.

"What do you mean you don't know?" I asked.

"I don't know what you mean." He hadn't looked up to meet my eyes, had kept digging, reaching his skinny tanned arms further and further and then inching his crouching body to the left, the direction of his work, when the reach of his arms was not sufficient.

His hair was long, tangles falling into eyes and I wanted to reach out and sweep it from in front of his face, tuck it behind his ears. I wanted to wash it and comb through it and get out the tangles, then brush and brush until I could see the shine. But I held my sweeping gesture back and instead whispered: "What do you mean you don't know what I mean?" It was starting to feel like an Abbott and Costello routine until I saw his eyes were shot with anger.

"I just don't," he answered adamant. He lived here with those girls, he went on. Sometimes an adult would show up, come to them from out of the woods, a woman. Sometimes two, a man and this same woman. He remembered times, though they were long ago, when more had been there, women and men, so that all the cabins were full. That had been something; there was always cooking and eating and laughing and screaming, and there had been other children too. The adults would sing and drink all night and sometimes there was dancing. The kids would all play games. The enchanted, where a child who was it tried to catch the other kids. When they were touched by this one they would have to stop dead in their tracks, only another free child could release them from their freeze, and like this it would go on until all the kids were caught, frozen stiff, dead in their tracks.

"Oh! The enchanted," I said.

Yes, that was what he had said. They would play hide and seek, too, in the edges of the woods. And sometimes the adults would get drunk and their screaming turned ugly and the children would grow scared. These big groups hadn't been here in a long time though. There hadn't been any large parties for a long time. But when they used to come they would show up in big cars, convertibles even, and one time one of the men had let him steer his car a little ways into the woods, and he had held his head very straight and high so that he could see in from his position there on this man's lap, see deep into the forest that these adults all came from. But, of course, he hadn't been able to see a thing for all those trees.

They would all spend the day swimming in the big shallow lake, the old ladies sitting under huge umbrellas.

"Nothing?" I asked.

Yes. That was the name of the lake. They never went in it without the adults, but when the adults were there, they swam and swam all day and then ate and danced at night. Some of the adults painted pictures, and taught them how to paint. Some sang and composed music and taught them how to sing: "Mary, Mary, Mary/ Merry, Merry, we/ Mary, Mary, Mary/ Marry, Marry, me/ If we all would go there/ then there we would be/ but for now we'll stay here/ and wait for you, me, we/ Mary, Mary, Mary…"

Now it was just that woman, and she sometimes brought a man. And though it wasn't as fun when she came alone or with a partner when she showed up she always brought gifts which the children kept hidden. Good food too. They would be there for a while, sometimes days, sometimes much longer; they'd kill one of the goats and roast it—or sometimes just a few chickens.

His voice went all hollow now, "We watch them do it," he said low and serious, "and sometimes they... sometimes we..." he stopped short, abrupt as if some external force, someone or something had told him to stop. He began jabbing at the dirt again. "Then they leave," he said. "After a while they always leave."

Manuel's digging became more insistent now as he went on; he speared his stick into the mud and sent big clumps up flying around him. The worst part was that while they were there the girls were different, became horrible with each other, he said. When there had been lots of adults, those big parties, this hadn't been a problem, but now that it was only ever just two the girls fought over them. Patricia, the littlest one, had cut herself once with a piece of broken glass and run to the woman and yelled 'Look, look, look at what Mona did to me!'

"That's my name too, you know."

"I know." He stopped his activity and impatiently lifted his eyes to me, "You already told me that."

"It's just that it seems strange to me. Everything you say is so strange and then when you say Mona it makes me think you are speaking about me."

He dropped his eyes and began furiously digging once again. "I'm not talking about you. Mona, the girl. She was blamed. The woman smacked her and yelled and Patricia secretly laughed and then she got all the attention for days, and of course it worked; she got a special present that time. The woman gave her a big ring. She wore it for a while and then she got scared we would steal it so she hid it somewhere. Probably in a hole, probably dug a hole for it. She likes to put things in holes."

"Why would you steal it?"

"I wouldn't!" He looked away, angry and red-faced.

"Who are these adults? Where do they come from? They can't actually live in the woods."

"You ask too many questions. You are giving me a headache big Mona. I want to sleep. I'm going to sleep."

He kicked at his castle, looked over at me while he yelled: "You gave me a headache, a big, big headache big Mona" and he stomped his whole creation to the ground. When the mud was all flattened to a little mound he ran into the third cabin. The one he slept in alone.

The enchanted

Francesca, Franc, the big girl, told me I could stay. She was dismissive in her invitation and I noted the intensity of her deep hazel eyes as she spoke. The smoothness of her olive skin stood out against the long and tangled black hair, and on her this mass of hair looked right, contrasting with and underlining instead of taking away from her delicate prettiness. I would sleep in her cabin, she pronounced. And as I listened to the harshness of her voice, I thought how her loveliness belied the toughness underneath, how because of her character I was only now starting to notice this prettiness.

There were three beds there and, of course, she got the biggest one, which sat right in front of, blocking, a big wooden door. "Closet" she answered my curious look. Franc told me I could choose from the other two beds. "Doesn't matter," she added. "They're the same."

I decided to sleep to the right of her.

I sat at the edge of my bed and asked, "Who are these adults Manuel told me about?"

She stared at me, direct and confrontational, for a while before she spoke: "It doesn't matter who they are big Mona. What matters is the fact that you hated your father's treats, despised his cakes. He made the best sweets for miles; why didn't you like them?"

"Who told you that, Franc?"

"It doesn't matter who told me that big Mona. What matters is that we don't scorn what we're given. Here we are and they do come and when they arrive they give us things. And we know how to appreciate what is offered to us. Not like you; your downfall is that you never knew how to be thankful."

"That isn't true. Stop speaking about me as if you know what you're talking about."

"Isn't that what you did to Manuel? Isn't that what you're trying to do to me? You're trying to figure just a little bit out so that you can pretend you understand what is going on around you. So that you can put us into one or two easy to handle sentences and then go off. It's not that easy big Mona. You will never understand. Other people are not so easy to comprehend. Simpleton."

It was while I sat on the edge of my bed staring at Franc all stretched out on her bed and unflinchingly staring back at me that little Mona walked in. "Can I sleep in here tonight?" she asked.

"I don't care," said Franc before she turned her back to me.

Mona crawled into the bed to the left of Franc and I got into mine; and then I tried to sleep.

I woke up in the middle of the night with little Mona wrapped around me. Her head lay in the crook of my neck and her small legs were draped over my own. I wondered at what point she had crept into my bed, what fears had driven her to me, a full stranger, in the middle of that dark night. I pushed her gently off of me so that I could settle back into my sleep, but as soon as I got her spread out on the other side of the bed she rolled right back over and put her arms around my chest. "Okay. It's okay," I whispered as I caressed her head, though I knew she was asleep and could not hear me. And then I closed my eyes exhausted yet even in that time of sleep I did not leave the children, for I dreamt of them and me there with them. We are there in the clearing in front of the cabins and we are together eating one of the chickens Franc has wrung dead, plucked clean and then roasted. And it is delicious. I have introduced them to my father's ashes and he sits among us. When we finish eating they get up and the two girls play with ropes while Manuel chases the little dogs who are busy chasing the chickens; Mona and I sit with my father and watch contented for a little while, and then Mona startles and begins to weep. I hear it then, the rumbling at the edge of the wood. "They're coming," Mona shrieks, and a line of terror shoots through me. The children all start wailing, surround me with reaching arms, but there is nothing I can do for I'm too terrified to move.

I awoke to Franc's harsh voice:

"You two look ridiculous, in that bed together. I've been up for hours now and there you both still lay. You really should get up." And with that Franc walked out of the cabin.

I was feeling panicky now. I wanted to figure it all out so I shook little Mona awake, "Wake up, Mona," I said.

"What? What do you want?"

"Tell me who the adults are who come to visit you four? What are they to you? Who are they?"

"I don't know big Mona. That woman just shows up and when she's here she plays with us, and sings, brings us good food and other things, all of what she brings delicious in some way. She makes a lot of promises, some of which she keeps. Sometimes she brings a man." She stretched her little arms up above her head, her back arching, her pouf of a belly coming out under her shirt.

"What kind of promises? What does she ask in exchange?" I looked at Franc's bed while I talked, then at the closet it sat in front of. "What's in there? Why does Franc block that door?" I could hear the panic in my own voice.

"It's a closet, silly. That's all it is."

"What's in it? Why does she block the door? Help me move her bed so I can see what's in it."

"No, Francesca will be mad if we do that. That's her stuff. She'll yell at me if I let you look in it. Why are you so jittery?"

"I won't tell her Mona; I won't tell her anything and I'll help you in any way I can. You can come with me when I leave and I'll take care of you."

"I don't need any help, silly. And I don't want to go anywhere."

"Forget it. I'll do it myself." And I leapt up and pushed the heavy bed aside and then pulled and tugged at the door with all my might till it opened. Mona sat on the bed we had shared and watched me frantically working.

"What is all this…?" It was stuffed full of beautiful clothing, silks, and organzas and brocades and rhinestone buttons on velvet coats with gold threading. There were thick wool capes and chiffon dresses and as I pushed through these—pausing to finger the dyed feathers and satins, the sequins and small pearls—I looked down and saw the shoes—a mass of buckles and laces and embossed designs on chunky, flat and tapered heels. While I was sorting through them all, there on the floor of that closet, I found a wooden box hidden in the left hand corner; and when I grabbed at it it fell open and out spilled a treasure of antique jewels. "What is all this?" I asked over-whelmed. "What is all of this stuff?"

"That's Francesca's. That's her treasure. You better put it all back just like you found it or she will get angry. Those things are hers."

"But what is it all?"

"Those are the things the adults gave her. Those are hers. We all have them," and here she became pensive, "though mine aren't as nice, and I don't have as much." And in a cheerful voice again: "But if you want to see I'll show you mine. Put hers away."

"Mona this is creepy. I think we should leave. I think you should come with me. Who is that woman and why do you want to stay?"

"What are you talking about big Mona? I can't go away. I, I don't want to go away. It's not like I couldn't if I wanted to, but I don't want to. Anyway, where would I go? And besides, she could come back soon and when she comes she will bring gifts and I want to see what she will have for me. She'll cook good food and I won't have to eat Franc's disgusting stews and we'll all sing and dance. I want to wait for my dresses and maybe there will be a necklace this time, or a ring like Patricia got," her face had gone all dreamy.

"Mona, I know how Patricia got that ring. I know what she did to herself to get it, how she blamed you. I'm going to leave today and I think you, you and Manuel, should come with me."

"Don't be silly. Silly. We don't need to go away." And she came over, pulled me out of the closet, and positioned me so that I would help her push Franc's bed back into place. I went limp, vacantly doing what this little creature asked me: "Push, silly."

"Get away from my bed." Franc was entering the cabin just as we'd gotten her bed into place. She darted Mona an angry look and I noticed the other two trailing behind her.

"We want you to tell us a story," Patricia demanded. "We also want more of that blue nail paint. Why do you look so scared, big Mona? Your heart must be positively racing. Wipe your palms on your skirt; why are they sweating? We just want a story. Come on, we'll all sit on Franc's bed." Franc nodded and at this gesture the other three climbed up. Franc took my hand and led me on herself, pushed Patricia out of the way so that she was now sitting next to me and then Patricia pushed little Mona aside and positioned herself on my other side. Mona and Manuel ended up at my legs, down by my feet.

"Okay." I breathed in and out three times, slowly. "Okay, I'll tell you a story," I paused for a minute more while I collected myself, and then I began: "There was a boy…"

"No," said Patricia. "That's not how you start a story. 'Once upon a time…' that's how you are supposed to start."

"She's right, you know," Franc added. "Do it right."

"Okay. Once upon a time. Once upon a time there was a boy… his name was Daniel. And, Daniel, along with a whole bunch of other boys was captured while in the middle of a game. Like help-less fish they were all gathered up in a big net by the king's men because he wanted these boys to be his and do his bidding at all times. So. So, he took them to the castle and held them in a tower but instructed his eunuchs to keep them happy and well fed. In fact, he told the eunuchs to feed them from his very own table, the royal meat, let them drink his very wine…"

"What's a eunuch?" interrupted Patricia.

"Well," I answered, "a eunuch is like a, a servant, you know, someone who helps the king."

"Oh."

"Okay, so the king tells his servants to give the children good stuff to eat and keep them happy. But Daniel says no, he will not eat the king's meat or drink his wine and he asks the head eunuch, who by now really loves him, to just bring him fruit and vegetables and water. And the eunuch, who adores Daniel so much he can't refuse him says, Okay but the king is going to be very angry if you don't grow big and strong like the rest of them, and then I will get it for allowing you to dwindle down to nothing. And Daniel says I know what I'm doing and I can only grow strong on my own, without the king's gifts. So like this he goes on for a while when one evening he and the only other three boys who have refused to eat the king's meat are allowed out for a walk by the lake with their friend eunuch guiding them. And it is a moonlit night and they look into the water and they see themselves there, stare at their reflections and see that they are strong and beautiful, and the eunuch too has to admit now that they have made the right choice refusing the king…"

"This is stupid," said Franc.

"You don't do that in the lake. You don't *look* in the lake. You swim in the lake. You splash and jump and dive," and Manuel started diving all over the bed, jumping up and diving again, and then pretending to splash, throwing his arms around on the surface of the bed, all of which angered Franc so that she kicked at him.

"Stop it!" She yelled.

"Yeah, Stupid. Stop it," and Patricia, who had her thumb in her mouth, kicked at him too.

Manuel ignored their kicks and giggled as he settled down. "Your legs are long, big Mona," he touched the skin lightly. "They're so smooth, and tan." He rubbed a little more decisively, then kissed my ankles, and down onto my feet.

"Do you have hair?" Patricia pulled her thumb out of her mouth and turned her face toward mine and looked me squarely in the eyes with the furrowed eyebrows of wonder.

"What?" I asked as I pulled my feet from Manuel.

"You know what I'm talking about. I know you do. Do you have hair? You do. You do have hair! I'm going to tell your boyfriend; I'm going to tell your boyfriend you have hair on your pee!"

"What are you talking about? I don't even have a boyfriend."

"When you get one, I'm going to tell him. You're going to kiss him and he's going to jump on you and you're going to rub all over him and I'm going to tell him."

"Your legs are pretty," little Mona said quietly. She looked up at me with a soft smile: "I like your legs."

"I like her arms," Franc added deliberately. She lifted my arm and exhibited it between her thumb and forefinger, "Look at her hands."

"Paint our fingers!" yelled Patricia. "Paint my toes!" and Franc dropped my arm.

Manuel started jumping on Mona and screaming "Do you have hair? Do you have hair on your pee?" Shoving himself on her and yelling into her face "Do you have hair?" humping on her little legs and asking "Where is your hair?"

I sat staring, noticed that my hands were clasping at the bedspread, and then Mona shrieked and tried to kick Manuel off. I shrieked. Franc and Patricia shrieked and then they all came in close and encircled me, hugging me very tight and bouncing up and down on the bed, shrieking louder and louder, until all their sharp shrieks joined forces and became one straight, piercing line.

"Shut up!" I yelled. "Be quiet."

They all turned on me. Dropped away from around me and pulled themselves back; and then they glared through cinched eyes like they had done the day before.

"We don't need to be quiet. Don't ever tell us to shut up," Franc pronounced. "No one told you you could go through my things big Mona." So she had seen. She stared at me with the eyes of an angry monarch: "I think you better leave now." And I could see she was trying to hold back the incensed tears.

"Yes. Of course. You're right." I glanced at little Mona, tried to catch her sweet black eyes so that I could convince her to come with me. But she decisively turned her face away. "You're right," I repeated.

"I'm going to tell your boyfriend you have hair!" I heard Patricia yell.

Their collective piercing laughter following me back into the depth of the dark woods.

A father revealed

Very soon I had left their clearing and was in a thick darkness, an undulating shade. And as I found myself once again in the midst of those dense trees a sense of deep defeat overwhelmed me and I slowed, their voices now just a thin din there in the distance—a whole world away. My legs grew suddenly heavy. Plodding, dragging steps. My eyelids dropped. My back folded itself down and over so that I had to work to keep myself upright. And then I quit working to stay erect—how much can one girl do?—and I fell down on all fours. I inched along on my knees and thought of penitents I'd seen in picture books or on tv, crawling to their shrines—bloody hands and knees evidence to the miles of their devotion—pushed on by guilt, or remorse, or hope; and with the image of them floating there before my eyes, I fell asleep.

How much can we flow through? How much must we endure before we are forgiven?

"Forgiven for what, big Mona?"

"For not looking, for never before having looked."

I see them there on the sand at the beach at the lake, the beach at Nothing. And I am there with them. It is a warm day, lovely, adorned by breeze, and we run to the water and plunge in, swim and splash for a long joyful time, and then, tired, make our way back to lie in the heat of the white sun. We close our eyes and like this we are settled and calm for a bit when I grow restless and decide I want to do something again. I get the idea to bury Mona and Manuel, up to their necks. They smile when I begin and then laugh as the warm sand piles on top of them, settles between toes and onto tummies and hands. "That feels nice," they say simultaneous and the other two giggle along as they look on. And then something shifts and I am shoveling the sand, fast now, on them, their faces and heads, suffocating; their bodies flail, little legs kicking, but I am faster than them, fierce, and can not stop. Franc and Patricia stand staring blank behind me. And then the two stop struggling and I sit back and look in horror at what I've done, powerless to change it now. I find that I am shaking and begin to weep and then they are gone from in front of me. And when I look around, frantic now, I see them again, alive, and I am confused but overjoyed. All four of them are there in front of their third cabin, the one I first saw them behind. And out from within this cabin comes Lily, Lily of the sweet jam, Lily with her long and flowing hair, and the now lively children surround her—encircle her in delight and when she offers them biscuits they don't throw them at the trees but take them from her in gratitude, near tears at their love of her as they eat from what she offers, there at her feet. And Lily does not make them grotesque in smeared blue, but instead gently combs out their hair and cleans off their faces, their elbows and knees. She kisses them and calmly tells them a story they do not hate. No, they love it, appreciate it—for it is about bunnies and kittens and such so that they listen to her, entranced. And then the twelve men are there too, Hans at the center, and the almost giant, and they too sit down at her feet. And when Lily is done with her tale these eighteen rise up together and dance and spin around in delight. It is in their spinning and happy laughter that I see my father. And I think: But he is dead, here in my bag. Yet there he is—walking up to them, and then there in their midst and they all hug and kiss at him and in their loving kisses he floats up joyfully before them, rising up—up—up….

I see myself. There I am at the edge of the woods! My heart fills with joy for I am there too and I run up to them and yell "Hey!" again "Hey!" But they do not seem to hear me. "What about me?" I ask. "That is my father. You do not know him. Come down Father! Come down. Show them that you are mine." But he does not look down at me. "You do not know him…

"He is my father," I repeated, eyes open now, heart beating fast. "You do not know him," I whispered to myself, the dream now fading, sweat dripping from my temples and my neck.

And then it came over me that there are things about my father… there are things. For instance, the fact that my father had once had a father too. That my father had taken my mother with him, but that he too had left something behind, the home he'd shared with his own recently dead dad, that last connection to place, to his father. His papa, a man he'd only mentioned to me once or twice.

All fathers have fathers but my father's father had barely known his. The old man was orphaned in youth. So my father's father had not been a good father, for he had never known a good father himself. My father, I know, suffered the results of his own father's lack.

Of my orphaned grandfather I had heard a mention, of my grandmother only that she'd died quite young…

(So many dead parents! Such a fact in his life that by the time of me, a mother's death slipped casual from his lips, punctuated only by slightly shaking hands.)

My grandfather, raised by a rich aunt, was a spoiled and lazy colonial grandson, for he himself was the offspring of Irish or Scottish stock—mixed, of course, as all Mexicans are, with the Indians who were already there. He was never around, drank a lot, was probably always searching for something himself so that he had nothing to offer my father; and my father had always had to take care of himself.

Some people say: I always took care of myself. But my father did. He actually did. He was a boy-man who figured things out on his own.

He was good with his hands and as a tiny boy sold woven bracelets and necklaces which he himself made out of multicolored string and pretty glass beads like an old Indian woman had shown him to do. She had done it once in front of the strange and curious pretty little boy while he watched with soft wide eyes and then she'd laughed as, with a thin and eager arm, he reached for some of her yarn. His small hands mimicked her skilled motions and when he had finished making his first bracelet she patted at his little tangled head and he beamed up at her with his long-lashed five year old pride. He sold them at the big noisy marketplace out of a little straw basket this woman gave him, and every week he would go and buy his yarn and beads from her and sit at her side where they wove in the silence of their work, he occasionally glancing over and then staring at her serious Indian face, her long black braids, she lifting her hand to pat at his head from time to time.

After more than a year of this quiet time of beads and yarn one of the older boys who wandered the marketplace one day came up and shoved him and brusquely told him that was sissy's work, what was he a fag?, and then with grimy fingers and a permanent sneer taught him how to do simple magic tricks to entertain the few tourists and all other adults of the small town. He would walk up to them at their lunch tables or as they sat lazily sipping at cold beer at one of the several outdoor restaurants which surrounded the main square, the Zocalo. Father did make more money with his speedy hands in this way and he loved the grown-up wonder and laughter he caused by making a peso disappear into thin air. This disappeared money would reappear at home where he gave some to his father and held on to the rest with which he bought their food.

He cooked this food he bought. He had learned how to cook very young, because if he didn't cook he and his father might not eat. There had been a woman—not a surrogate mother, but a woman—whom my grandfather had brought home one cold night. I brought her home for you, my grandfather had once slurred at my father, but this woman with her taut and angry arms, tight hard body and grimacing missing-toothed face, had not liked my father and she didn't get much of anything from my grandfather, not love or even affection which is what we imagine she must have most wanted from him, but not money either which would have probably been just fine too. So when my father was six or seven or such, she had gotten fed up and gone out on her own. "Tell your father he is a disgrace," she'd turned and hissed at the boy as she shoved his head with her bony hand and then scurried briskly out the door of that once beautiful, now decrepit, colonial home.

She had taught him to cook though, or, rather, my father had learned by sitting very still in the corner of the kitchen—he knew not to disturb her, for, The Ugly, that is what he secretly called her, The Ugly didn't mind raising her hand to him, and so he sat silent—silent and watching what The Ugly did with her fast and able hands. How could someone as hateful as her make such delectable food? There must be something in her, if hidden deep down deep within; there must be some small bit of warmth and good will with which she created such wonderful sense-delighting dishes. And after she left for good, my father mimicked her moves—chopping and mashing, boiling and frying—as he had done just a few years before with the Indian woman of the serious face and dyed yarn bracelets.

His father never thanked him. Not for the coins, which my father left piled by his pants there on the chair. Not for the rice and soups and various stews which my father put on the table every night. Not for being a boy man who didn't ask for anything and who gave, gave, gave like a Saint, or a masochist, or a very sad and unloved child. My father working and doing, his little nimble hands making things, magic things, happen, all of this from out of nothing.

By the time he was nine he started finding real work, picking fruit with those very quick hands on a ranch one town away. Pounding intricate designs into tin at a tinsmiths two towns away. Through this tinsmith he met a man who made paper machiêr masks three or four towns away and in whispered secrecy this man offered Father more money than the smith. The tourists who came to his shop would like the sight of the skinny, hard-working boy, their pity pushing them to bigger and bigger purchases, this mask-maker knew. And so like this my father started to wander the land, over mountains and through valleys, town to town, job to job. But he always came back to his own town so that he could spend at least some time with his father. Look at his face, and wonder at his depths. Cook for him a bit.

By the time he was fourteen my father had made it to Acapulco, on the back of a truck, with two or three other boys from his small town, the one of the magic tricks and permanent sneer having convinced them all to hitch along. They rode back there, their tanned skin crackling in the sun, their joshing shoving laughter carrying them along.

The sneering magic trick boy's older brother was a front desk clerk at one of the big hotels and he got them all jobs as bellhops, feet trained to run forth at the sound of clink clink. Of this time I've seen a picture: my father young and strong with big beautiful eyes, a shy smile and those long legs of youth, standing straight and proud with puffed chest on a cliff, the lissome salty sea spreading spreading, out below him.

This is a time that I've heard of, a time he could be prodded to speak of in detail, a happy time: My father learning broken English from the tourists and drinking in the sun and the cheap beer. My father having reached the ocean on his own, running around with other bellhops, wild with the breath of possibility and his own strength at having reached.

In that picture I can see that his eyes shine with the light of his own self, the fire of opportunity.

To the rescue

He is lying under the shade of a palm frond umbrella, propped up on a lounge with his upper chest and head shielded from the sun, there in the thick summer heat of that crowded beach. This is an Acapulco of mostly Mexican tourists, Americans sprinkled sparingly between. Though snaking themselves between these thousands of vacationing bathing suit bodies are the countless hard-toil men and women for whom it never ends; work is now and ever and always and so they approach insistent carrying their wares, coconuts employed in every possible way: with a straw for drinking or in chunks for eating or as oil for rubbing on your body to help that tan and smell so good. Men sell colorful hammocks too, though no room to hang them here, and women carry tiny shell figurines of dogs or fish or cats, coral necklaces and pretty earrings, three or four in each hand, and they look you in the eye and walk toward you authoritative as if you've already purchased what they've got. So don't even glance at them, he has been warned, though he does not heed. Not a man to look away, he takes everything in, and as a result has a big pile of souvenirs to carry home there at his side. And there are what must be a million children running in and out of lapping water and screeching back and forth and the teenage girls have long black hair, sinewy sea-salt dripping whips. Dressed in white not a drop of sweat waiters appear right when he needs them and bring him more and more beer for just one of those coins, so inexpensive he gives a tip of two. And he is happy if a bit lonely surrounded by that crowd, propped up, looking on—the observational eye—from under his umbrella, when from that shade he sees my father. He sees the boy shyly taunting and laughing with the other rougher six. He stares at their open laughter, gazes at the prodding, flailing limbs, emphatic tossing of arms, playfully kicking joyful legs. Those boys are a loosely defined group, some coming others going, shoving each other pretty roughly and running in and out of waves. The older two or three look direct and confrontational at every girl that walks their way while they hungry gulp from sweating beers. But he looks familiar, that boy, the quietest one on the edges of the group. Yes. He has seen him at his hotel. The bellhop. That one with the big eyes and shy laugh is the boy who carried his bags up to his room. "Come here boy," he says to my father at the beach.

Father walks up to the American who's called out to him, pointing at himself and with his eyebrows raised up in the form of a question, Who me? his eyes ask. "Ah, I know you," says my father in his broken English before the man has a chance to speak. And today he is feeling nice and easy so he goes on with his chat: "You gave me a good tip," he nods. "But you made me work for it," my father adds. And then he rubs at his arm, at the muscle, "Still hurts," he jokes.

The man laughs and then he asks my father questions about his work, his family, his life. And finally he asks the most important of the questions: "Have you studied," the man asks, "don't you want to learn a trade?"

Father said no to the first and yes to the second of those two questions with a gentle nodding of the head. So this man took him to the US on his return, to attend high school in a big city far away.

He stayed there for two years. For Father already had a way of living. He had a way of wandering from town to town and two years in this man's home—with rules of when to get up and where to go, what to do and how to think and how to be and when to act—were enough. All this imposed structure did not seem worth more than the two years it took my Father to learn some skills and to speak in a new tongue.

Or perhaps it was that he missed his own father, my grandfather. Or one of a million other possible reasons, something about the quality of the sun. And so, enveloped in the mystery of his motives, he snuck out of his bedroom window one dark night and hitched and walked his way back to his own town, where he arrived filthy and wild-eyed after his week's voyage of backward retreat.

This too is my father, so that he had not just been the man of the intense love of my mother, the sorrowful longing for her after she'd gone. He had been a young man who had eyes that others took in, who made choices and wandered and yearned and laughed and explored. He had not just been the sad and heavy father I had known.

It is sometimes hard for me to remember all of this.

The American

Someone had done it for him. That's the answer. For we've asked ourselves: why would this man, this American, offer to take this youth with him, to his home, to feed and clothe and educate? I know what you are thinking, have gotten to know you a little bit and know what your mind has already ventured to. But no, there was really none of that (and if there was, that kind of longing was kept hidden deep within). In fact, someone had done it for him. This generosity had saved his own life. He said he wanted to return the favor, complete the circle, perhaps set a new one rolling.

He was one of those orphans, street kids, who in the early twentieth century had been plucked off the alleys of New York City and sent off on a train to fill out the households of middle America. Most of them didn't fare well, were taken willingly, yes, papers signed in exchange for a new child; yet were treated not as children, but as something to which we will not put a word and used as extra hands on a farm, or a store or a mill, fed hardly at all so as to maximize profit, minimize expense, clothed in empty feed sacks which stingy wives stitched together to look like real clothes. And as for learning, books? What on earth was a book?

For these children the freedom of the streets had been much better than this. The charitable rich ladies who'd gathered them up and sent them off would not ever come to understand that the freedom of their running fierce, of their snatching food from stores or outdoor carts, the freedom of their petty thievery and small gangs and wild into the night games was looked back on by this unlucky bunch with the melancholy of the good old days. And their wise little minds' eyes must have seen it coming, for the train ride to these new homes was viewed by every single one of these children as a solemn affair. Even the toughest older three sat teary eyed, racing hearts leading them into the unknown. Unsure hands clutching at the bags which those fancy ladies and city officials had provided for those whom they'd pridefully told themselves they had saved, before boarding them together on that one train and waving them off with their pomp. The children's stiff bodies and darting eyes revealing them to passersby as they hung tight to those satchels which held an extra dress, a pair of shoes, a bible, a comb, and maybe a hat.

And then in the midst of their new lives their muffled in the middle of the night cries—muffled because if you don't shut up I'll beat you—filled out the American landscape. Only the beautiful plains animals and the spirits of long ago massacred Indians knew how to make out the language of those muted cries, lifted their heads solemnly in recognition of a new set of the white man's sins. And then, one day, all of their crying abruptly stopped—for there was no use in it and each and every one of these children, living their separate, isolated, and miserable lives had in the same instant suddenly remembered from their days there on the streets of New York that to get by you must be hard. Yet, and this was not a common occurrence for most of them, if you were to look at them with the slightest bit of tenderness, ask a question in a soft voice, inquire after their mothers or fathers, even after forty or fifty years, their grown up eyes would well up, their tough features would melt away and they would become puddles of tears at the flood of sad memories, their dreary lives, and at the softness in your voice, at your capacity to be tender with them, at the realization that these things, tenderness and softness, these sweetest of things, do in fact exist.

Those hard shells are thin, we know.

But the American, our American, was one of the lucky ones. They'd taken him in as one of their own; had they had their own this is how they would have treated them. And they beautifully clothed him, and they schooled him well and he learned to love books, and they fed him—but this could not be food! these meats and these breads and these pies were not food. He had eaten food on the streets of New York and this was not it. This was heaven itself in his mouth, paradise itself that he ate.

And it was by watching her that he learned. By watching his mother, for this was what she'd patiently waited for two years to have him call her; she'd made it understood that it was a possibility when he'd meekly stepped off of that train with two other boys who were meant for that vicinity and then the boys stood by the inspector who read out all three names. She walked up to claim him, having months ago memorized his name from there on her official letter. And now there was not just this letter but a boy before her, this actuality, this little boy who stood now there in front of her on that platform shyly looking down as she told him that one day he might come to call her mother, "That is what I feel I am to you now" she'd said as she took from him the small bag full of his belongings—until that moment all he had in the whole world; and it was by watching her, Mother, that he had learned to cook.

He not only watched, but he asked questions and he wrote down—for at his school he had learned not only to read but to write too and though he really did like reading this was the only form of writing he enjoyed—so he wrote down recipes which no one had written down before. "How much pepper?" or "flour" or "pork" he'd ask and she would have to slow down and measure and weigh, for her people kept all of this in their heads. He wrote it all down and he imitated her and at first it all came out so badly and this funny once-orphaned child—our American—would make his mother laugh.

The husband, the father, wanted the boy to go on with his school, to study numbers, or law, or something abstract. But the American only liked food, that which he could create from a pile of this and that and combine and turn into something delicious and new, all of these scattered things, when put together and carefully measured and mixed and baked and tenderly treated could give birth to something wonderful and new. Yes, something real that he could touch and smell and taste. And the father and mother were good and knew not to push a boy from becoming the kind of man he wanted to be. You mustn't kill the spirit—that American spirit—before it has a chance to find itself.

Nearly fifty years later, his own parents long dead—for they had not been young when they'd taken the American in—he was on vacation at a Mexican resort. He saw a boy whose shy humor had reminded him of his own. He saw a skinny long-lashed big-eyed boy and thought of himself on the streets of New York.

He picked my father much as he had once been picked. Then he took the boy and he taught him how to bake. My father didn't much like school, except for the English that it taught him and the writing that he learned. But to go and spend afternoons at his bakery with the American... to watch him sift and knead and mold. To watch and see and learn and then to be allowed, encouraged even, to do, just for the pleasure of the doing... this was worth the 2,000 mile trip. This was worth leaving that paradise by the sea.

And the American laughed with my father, at his magical quick learning hands, much as his mother had once laughed with him. "Good work, boy" he would say after a day in the bakery, "Good work."

My father would go back to his own town at seventeen, a baker, a candy maker. He would sneak out of the window of that American's house and make his way back to his town, where he would make the most magical treats, the treats that in time would lead him to my mother, or she to he.

When the party's over

My mother couldn't believe her eyes. Mara could not believe her eyes. They were all asleep. They were all asleep! He had been right. The baker had been right! And now they were all actually, undoubtedly, and verifiably asleep. She ran from one to the other, from long table to long table, heart racing, limbs flying, finally pulling herself just a little bit together and daring with careful gentle hand to touch some of those towering curls, the stiffness of that womanly hair. With her cautious fingertips she caressed the silks and laces, inspected earrings and mustaches. She pursed her lips at the loveliness of all those jewels. And her heart began once again racing, running in her chest as she ran between, and paused and looked down at a group and then jerkily moved on to the next set of sleeping bodies slumped over each other, their tables and chairs. Piles of guitars and violins on the floor, the mariachis with heads on instead of in their big sombreros using them like some kind of stiff urn pillows.

Then she found the prettiest young girl, much prettier than herself she thought, though she knew her mother would not agree and she poked at this girl's golden skin a bit, ran her curious finger up and down her arm. She would have liked to have been friends with her, her green velvet dress was the loveliest at the whole ball. They could giggle together over jokes only they understood and they could flirt with all the boys at that party and at all other parties too, dance with only each other knowing, of course, that this would make all that young male blood boil, and Basta would not be in the picture at all for this was a dream, her dream, and she and this girl would be friends. They would go for walks in the Zocalo, would parade around, arms hooped together and the other girls would be jealous and the boys would march up and dare to say a word, just one word, to which the two would roll their eyes and giggle and then the boys would lurch off and then new ones would strut up and try their darndest to impress. And they'd sit alone at cafés and get ice creams served in beautiful crystal bowls and they would not really eat their ice creams at all but just roll their silver spoons longingly about all over them and they would let their eyes get heavy with their sultry daydreams and whisper wishes and desires over those lazy spoons.

She woke up out of her intense new friendship and saw, confirmed that, yes, they all kept sleeping, silent, not a snore. And there was Refugio Basta; she decidedly stomped over and prodded at his face a bit, poked him near his eye, and then laughed, tossing arms fluttering down to rest at her sides. It had worked; Basta didn't budge. And her mother, there was her lovely mother, asleep; she glided smoothly over and then she reached down and arranged her mother's long red skirt. The whites of her eyes were showing from under her lids and Mara passed her hands before them once or twice. Then she lowered her head slowly and kissed at her brow, then down by her lips.

Asleep.

All of them asleep.

She looked up and wanted to dart between them more, to touch at this and that one, maybe try on those pretty gold shoes, but then she thought that she should hurry, gather up her things and go.

But what were her things? Where was her bag? Would she really need her bag? What would she need? There was nothing so important in her bag, just some powder and a comb, and then she saw it, focused her eyes upon it, that stupid little bag there at the foot of her chair, there on the platform, at the center of the head table. She gasped at the awakened realization that this had all been done for her. That if she had not met that baker boy she would be married the next month. And then she shuddered and pulled herself together.

Mara ran out, tip-toed first so as not to wake them, but then remembered they were as dead to the world and ran out of that hall making as much noise as a hundred pound girl of sixteen can possibly make.

And there was Father. Out by the tree down the road, just where he'd said he would be. It had been a while now since he'd seen the waiters come out and gather the men who had been lounging and smoking outside all around the large hall, and he had said to himself, Yes, the girl has done it. Little Mara has done it. And then he'd stood waiting outside the party hall which Basta had had built on his ranch fifteen years before, a private party hall, a conceit, half a mile from his big house, the big mirrored baroque hall which my father had heard of but never seen. He waited out-side praying that it would go well, for just five minutes after the men were called in, and then his mind started racing forth and then stopping itself at the thought of every soon-to-come possi-bility. He would marry sweet Mara. Stop. He'd kiss her, fall slowly toward her and then plant himself firmly on her full, delectable lips as soon as he got her onto the burro's back. Stop. She'd wrap her beautiful long thin arms around him in gratitude and then he'd hoist Mara onto the beast and then get on himself in front of her and turn his face toward her, turn his whole body toward her and push up on little Mara and kiss, yes, he would even open his lips, stick his tongue in her mouth, dart it in and out a bit. Stop. He'd gently touch, with tactful fingers, at her neck, down her shoulder then slide over and in toward her breast where he'd feel the soft and giving flesh. Stop. He rolled his hand into a fist and then punched at his leg, at his arm, his chest. He was near tears at his frustration, at his desire for the girl, for even a fantasy of the girl, an unself-censored fantasy in which he could act out the love he felt for Mara without making himself stop. Act out the longing he felt in his bones. The decisions he'd made, the risks he was willing to take. But then he'd known it would be soon so he'd stopped punching at himself, breathed in and out so his erection had subsided and rushed back the way he'd come, over half a mile away where he'd left the burro tied up to the post of a fence.

And here he'd been, under the branches of this big tree, for the last twenty minutes, heart beating fast, praying again, but no longer allowing even a censored fantasy, worried that maybe one or two of the guests had not taken a bite of his treats, that this was what was keeping the girl. He imagined her anguish. Why are those two not asleep? Tears of fear running down her face. How does she get out of that? Should he go rushing in? He should have brought a weapon, a knife, maybe he could find a big stick, his eyes darting about, looking, looking for something, anything he could use.

But presently he saw her, running wildly out and his heart sped fast not with worry now but with excitement, with the triumph of it having come together so well and then also with the sight of his Mara, beautiful, sweet, running Mara.

There.

There she was.

To ride and ride and ride

But she is crying. Has tears in her eyes. Running down her cheeks? Her hair is sticking to her face, sticking to her neck, long strands of sticky bathed in her own tears.

No. No, little Mara. Do not cry. I am here. Right where I said I would be. Let me see. Let me just pull out my handkerchief; I swear that it is clean. See. I washed it myself, put it on the line. There. Let me dab at your chin and your cheeks and your eyes. Don't toss your head. You are so lovely. Look at you in your white party dress, in your lovely party dress. Your sweet beaded bag, it's so tiny, a little bag dangling like a bracelet from your wrist. Why are you gasping for air? Breathe in. Deeper. Breathe in and out. Again.

I am here. Oh, no, do not cry.

His head tossing and turning, hands wringing, he managed to calm her just a little bit. Then he calmed his own hands and he put his arms around her; but this was not what he'd imagined when he'd dreamt of the solemnity and sweetness of the first time he would have his arms around her frame. These heaving shoulders and chest, gasping for air. What is that sound? That brutal gasping sound. From her? Could that horrible sound be coming from her?

Come on, Mara. He patted at the back of her head and shushed, shushed, shushed her. We have to go, he whispered to her. We have to get started, to get as much distance as we can. He moved her gently out away from him, held her at arms' length and tried to look into her eyes, to communicate the gravity of what he was about to say through a profound stare: They'll be asleep for three days, but we have to make sure that we're far, far away from here when they wake up from their slumber.

So he got her on the burro, all dreams of absorbing kiss and sultry caress buried deep below the worry that her tears and lugubrious expression had caused to grow like a high wall between them. How could he feel what he felt, be happy at its having all worked, elated at his having her here, when she gave off nothing but misery and loud, anguish-filled sobs?

Nevertheless, they start riding, riding, riding. He's stuffed a blanket with sweaters, clean clothes; he even bought her some things, a dress and flat shoes, then rolled it all up and tied it to the back of the saddle. He's got woven bags and baskets full of food and canteens of water tied to and hanging from the blanket's sides. When they get to the river border they can leave the burro.

He lived over there, in that land, for a while, two years actually, so he knows the language. Will be able to maneuver them quite well. "We'll go to Texas, which is right across, or better yet to California which is where I lived with that American." The Texas border should be in four and a half days' ride, and then they can decide. He's got a big wad of pesos he's been saving for almost three years and when they get to the US he'll go work in a bakery and then soon he'll be able to open his own. "It won't take long," he assures her, "no one knows how to bake like me." A bit of shining pride, the second time he's let her see it. We'll buy a little house. Me and you. He tries to make his voice jolly, as he tells her all of this. Lifts his hands off the reins and turns toward her as he points and motions to show her how he rolled everything up inside that blanket, secured it to the saddle, tied the bags to its side. He tells her the burro's name is Paco. Smacks at the beast's big thigh a bit and tells her he's had him for two years. A good and loyal friend. They used to ride out together at least once a week; he'd take the day off and they would ride sometimes to Rio Mara. "Are you named after it; is that where you got your name?" he asks before he goes on. To the river where he would swim and float while Paco looked on, sometimes lowering his head into the water, to drink from the cool wet just a little bit. Or sometimes they would ride to the green valley past the river where Paco would eat the long grass as he himself lay under the big olive tree thinking up new recipes, new ways of making things. This is where he'd thought up many of the treats for her... Paco would decide when it was time to go, he says: Come over to me and nudge with his nose when he was full, and then I'd climb up and we'd ride back in early dusk, the sky big and wide and sometimes red, groups of birds squawking up into that sky and then falling gentle but noisy back into their trees as we rode by, me melting into the rhythm of Paco's slow and steady gait. Like we were one, our bodies merging, his burro body and my human body becoming enveloped by something bigger than the two of us, us one with it and with each other too. Just like this, Mara, with you, now, also.

And at this the girl, who had seemed subdued, gave a big, deep, heaving cry: Mamiiiii, she wailed. Mamiiii, again.

The stop of the flow

He wasn't the type to get angry. Or, rather, he wasn't the type to show it when he was. But he did begin to get angry. He'd worked so hard, was still working so hard, talking talking, soothing soothing, trying to get the girl to stop her wailing; he'd planned and worried and given everything up and now that he should be allowed to feel good, like what he'd done had been the right thing, she was taking it away from him. His bones were starting to feel like jelly; he was turning into a rubber man. He was scared that he would lose his determination. They were not done here, had a long voyage to make and they had to be strong. They had just started and those tears were wearing him out. So, he did get angry. But he did not fully show it though he did tell her, and not with the soft and dreamy voice he'd been using up till then, he did tell her that she had to stop her crying. She was getting Paco all wet. And what did she want? She could not possibly want to go back. Did she know what that would mean? Did she want to go back and marry that Basta? To go back and deal with that life? Yes, yes, of course he understood the loss of a mother—even one who would offer her daughter up thus, he added in a quieter voice—of her mother, yes, but remember Mara, little Mara, Marita, what that life was. And here his voice got tough: Remember the reality, what your mother was in fact leading you to, and that will help to remind you that we have to go on.

My mother stared at the back of his head as he continued to talk. Nobody had ever told her not to cry before. Nobody had ever said—we have to go on; no one had ever given her an option for a future, a we that she could feel she was a part of; but then, of course, whether he was aware of it or not, he had only partially offered this gift, for he'd already negated the we with a command, with a restrictive order, with a: Stop your crying. You're getting the burro all wet. And then the way he went on and on about her mother. It mortified and made her angry, both at the same time. She had to turn her face away. And so she looked out at the land-scape. Away from the back of his head and out at the vastness of this land. Herself a nothing in the midst of it. The opposite of what he had said. The opposite of a union with it like he and Paco had once had—for she was a black hole. And her story was a dark gray formless mass now, a mass that could not be identified as anything, that could not even take the shape of the tears which had given meaning to her past.

And not knowing how to fight for this thing he'd given then immediately taken, for this space inside a we, she instead did what she did best and pulled it all inside her. With one last long sigh then gasp then sigh, she pulled it all in and then in a gesture as extreme as that which she was feeling, she stopped all of her crying.

And she never shed another tear again.

Not in front of him.

3:
Manolo makes shoes

A brother found

Here I was. And out there, somewhere, was he. And nights were long and days were blurred, an unclear story between us.

As I walked back toward the street it seemed somehow different, even from a distance. I approached and then pushed through the gate which marked the entrance to that trail; I'd been backtracking toward it for days, out of the forest, and as I crossed that sick threshold I stepped back onto the street my father and I had looked down upon two and a half decades ago from what would soon come to be our back yard. "We're back," I whispered to him. His ashes. The light was falling now, but it was much more than the play of this dim light that made it all seem different. A shift had come, though on that day I still scarcely knew what it might be. And the trees seemed to have grown, particularly the Chinese elms and sycamores which I could see peeping out high above my fence, so that there was a sense that some of the wilderness of those dark woods had followed us back home.

When I approached my house I saw the cat, sitting, waiting patient on the stoop. He was thin and bedraggled. Grey and messy with huge entreating yellow eyes. Poor old Fluffy, I whispered, guilt at his shabby state spreading deep inside. Good old cat, I said a bit louder as I bent and picked him up, rubbed about on his head; and while I unlocked the front door he nuzzled his chin into my arm, lightly nipped at my left hand, then sniffed about at my satchel and my father inside it.

It was in receipt of that gentle love bite, the feel of that sniffing nose, that I fell apart. For even if my search had been indirect and convoluted, a lame and laughable quest, I had tried to do my father's bidding. Of course it had all been tainted from the first, but it was only now becoming obvious that it was impossible for me to go on with the game. For how could I move forward after the silencing of my mother? Once I'd gotten to the point where my father had told Mara not to cry? Because if I was to keep going with my version for much longer I would have to come up with her death; that was the only thing left in that story, besides our birth, and I was not ready to imagine all of that. None of my fanciful fabulist reading had prepared me for how to manage that. The heart stopping; instant death. Me and my brother there in our crib, and then a month later he is gone too.

Or the other version I'd heard whispered a few times… had had to face directly just that once… much more terrifying than her death… mother there one day, and then the next: a stealthy sick escape, bundled in each arm a little babe… no, only one… that anxious muffled cry not mine. At the stifled sound my father stumbles sleepy to window, witnesses her quick depart… sees her covering my brother's mouth as she runs past, hears her anxious murmurs, shushing soft and low… he understands and does not lift a hand. He can't.

How could I ever finish that story? Pick a suitable ending? There was none, for every possible version made me sick.

And so I walked into the house instead and with the hope of scattering my ghosts flipped on all the lights. Bright now, I made my way into his bedroom and tossed my father on his bed, though a part of me felt like flinging him against the wall instead. I still largely blamed him for the mess that was me.

If only he had been a better liar, had kept his secret safely guarded… had thought to move us far away from here and remnant whispers… or had chosen not to speak at all before his death.

I pulled myself away from him and dragged my legs to my room, my desk, where I turned the computer back on. I placed the cat on my lap and while I forced myself to read my piled up e-mails I brushed out those long grey mattes. Poor old Fluffy, I murmured again. Good old cat.

But as I tried to focus on the screen in front of me I found it impossible to pay attention and my stomach turned acidic; because I'd been rushing in mad circles my whole life and all I had to show for it was what had gotten me going in the first place: a deep sense of confusion, basic questions never answered, never to be cleared up, for I was a centerless one. I could never speak direct. In my life there was no clear and direct plot, straight storyline, an a to b with a beautiful narrative arc.

I ran my hands through my hair and wondered if hers had been like mine, long and often messy, full of waves that never quite turned into curls. I stretched out my legs and pulled off my tights, looked at my toes and closed shut my eyes. I knew I finally felt like action, a change, understood that at some level even if I didn't know how to accomplish it myself, I wanted to make sure that something happened, so I decided to hire someone out there—in the real world—whose specialty it was to speak direct. Clear without restraint. Say things firmly and then show facts. I did a bit of searching and found him quick: an internet private detective. I filled out some forms, agreed to pay a large sum, and then slowly I typed in my name, date of birth, hospital account, favorite food, last read book, my dress size. I then turned everything off and went to bed.

And within the week my detective had moved me out of my life-long misty and inexpressible doubt—extravagantly adorned by that soft if fallible cushion of tall tale—and dropped me flatly down into the stark unpadded harshness of real life. He had a full report. Manuel goes by Manolo, it read. He makes shoes in New York. Spent his early life in London with your recently dead mother (and here my heart fully stopped before my body again began and I released a loud gasp) and an English hairdresser he calls Dad.

I yanked the letter from my eyes.

My detective

had not even found my brother yet, and already I was coming up against things I did not feel strong enough to take on.

The sun fell, rose, fell, rose, maybe three times. It was on this third or fourth cycle that I began registering sound again. A car door first. A male voice, loud, my neighbor yelling for (at?) his wife. Minutes or hours or eons later a squirrel, barking. Old Fluffy's yowling cry, territorial display, not quite a full fight.

A hummingbird twitter.

A swaying blade of grass.

At Fluffy's deep throated cry I had managed to lower the arm holding the letter and I now made my way to the dining room window, the sun falling; I pawed at the glass with my empty left hand, pressed my face against the pane, took in those soft pink clouds shifting on that incredible endless blue sky, a splendor we get at the beginning of the best of our smog-filled Los Angeleno early nights. The golden hour. That light. The colors intermingling and moving and changing, slow and gentle transformation, and the beauty in that. It's time to let go, I whispered, as we hurtled sure and deep into the darkening early evening light.

I made my way back to the package and pulled out everything it had.

My detective had gotten me copies of our birth certificates. I held them in my hand, those irreversible and irrefutable documents which I had never seen, and there he was, my brother Manuel, and there she was too, alive, having filed for those papers the week after we'd come out, the two of us.

It hit me then, the gravity of my father's lie. I'd grown up more than half believing I had somehow killed my mother, my birth her death. And my fear that my anger—the search for facts fueled by this anger—might kill him was tied in with that death. As was my continual inability to act: I had wandered dusty edges and shadowed corners as a child and adolescent, had attempted college—never finished—had no ambition and so of course no real job, my romantic life was a sham. For I had always already done the undoable, the most heinous act: matricide. I was Electra and her brother both, hounded by the furies, running from my life. My mother dead in childbirth, and it wasn't until he was nearly dead too that he took that grave lie back. And though there had been times when I'd suspected none of it was true, I could never really challenge… but my mother had signed, here was her hand on that paper. And I wanted to beat my father for the sick effects of his lie.

The sense of peaceful resolution I'd had before opening that package vanished and I now ran to full rage. I did not even feel it rising up inside me and now I flew around the house fuming, poor Fluffy apprehensive and shakily taking cover under this piece of furniture until seeing me descending and scurrying to that. And then I would pause, for whole minutes at a time, thoughts rushing through my mind, colliding with each other, for this meant that everything must be a lie; she had in fact only recently died, the detective's letter said. So what could I trust? My mind started racing again, over all that he had told me about her, all that I had heard spilling from his lips, but immediately it was too much, so I stomped again, rushing through the house, before pausing and once more trying to draw something up, times he might have said things that could be counted as facts. And then, No, I had to stop again. Blank my head out and move, run, stop, and pace, stop, and move again.

And then after a day or two of this, exhausted by this marching, by this whole shifting of emotions, I finally walked back into his bedroom and stood before him. I thought about what makes most ordinary people lie, then. What has driven most all of my lies. Fear, or sadness. A misled desire for attention, or love, that lonely, heavy heart. The monstrousness of the darker emotions ample fuel for all my fabrications. My own dishonesty has not usually, almost never, really, been driven simply by spite.

And then I see him take form and rise before me from out of that bag, imagine myself yelling at him, releasing all my self-hatred and deep fury upon him, and in response: that pained and awkward smile of his, those slowly lifted heavy, confused and sheepish eyes. How could I tell you she had left us? my father asks. I could not bear to think it to myself, so what words could I have used to tell you that?

I pulled my eyes away from him there, floating before me.

Why was I always so angry at my poor dejected dad?

Forgiveness for my father comes much easier now that he is gone, when he does not need it, cannot do anything with it, my pardon.

I dragged myself back into the front room, slumped into the over-wrought burgundy armchair, and, finally, openly cried.

With swollen eyes I stared at her shaky hand on my birth certificate. Imagined the same unsure fingers which had once held that pen now running through my hair. I dropped the weight of my head down into them and let those spectral digits work their way about my scalp. She was really dead now, and I had never seen her face, never held her hand; and somehow the thought that I could have (I could have smelled her hair, placed my face deep in it and caught a scent of perfumed neck), made everything else seem much worse. And now, too, I realized I had to really begin to think of her leaving, to directly wonder a new question which was: why had she left? And by extension: why had she left me?

I can't answer that, she said. Her hand now gently tugging at some strands of my long hair. I could never answer that. I was unhappy. No, not unhappy, miserable. I was blind. I was selfish. I was lonely. I was sad. I was scared. I was confused. I was hopeful. I was terrified. I was going mad. I was a woman. I was seventeen and I was already a woman and I cannot answer that.

I am not strong, I whispered back. I am weak and I am frightened. Shameful, a disgrace. I know my father too was unhappy confused scared miserable blind selfish. Lonely. He was an unclear and fuzzy man. Yet I went right along with him, became a part of that blurred mass, even after I had for a long time, at some level, suspected that you'd left. I made myself not think it, because what kind of a mother leaves her child, a baby, not yet one? And so I became one with my father and I too have been a liar, because leaving only happens in death, I silently concurred. That is the only way you could have gone.

I'll find Manuel, now, and talk to him. I can finally go and do that.

She lifted her hand off of my head then; and my mother was gone.

What to write

I stood up on shaky legs, warily bunched the birth certificates and the printout of my detective's findings and set them face down on the desk for another full week, a week of heart stoppings and loud gasps, long, barely audible sighs. And in this week of not looking I made actual the emptying of my old self to make room for something new by emptying the house. I went through his clothes, those great big shirts and pants, underwear. My father's underwear. I put it all into huge black plastic bags. I wiped up the months since he died old dust, then below it the grime that had been building for my whole life before that, swept aside the dirt, mopped. I re and re and re-arranged the furniture and then decided I would throw most of it out. I wanted a clean house. An empty house. A minimalist house with few chairs and adorned only by the strange cactus flowers you can find growing on our hill. I squeegeed the windows so the light came in clear now, like it had those first few months in this house, before our lives made them opaque. I opened some of them, stuck my head out of one and saw the neighbor's gardener and called out to him, the first person I'd talked to in a very long time. He lowered his leaf blower, came over, and for fifty bucks helped me to throw all the old junk out. We worked silently and then before leaving he asked if he could keep some of what I called trash. Of course, I said as I handed him his fee.

I'll be back to pick it up with my truck, he said as he enclosed the bills in his hand.

I moved into the kitchen then, and I threw out all of Father's mixers, and baking dishes, and nutmeg graters. I threw out bags and bags of aged flour and jars of cinnamon and little bottles of vanilla and a single very small plastic container holding strange and tiny baking mushrooms, for depth and rest, the label read. I threw out all the tools he'd used in the overly sweet almost daily stirring up and evocation of the woman who had long ago left him, my mother. I threw it out and put it in the bin myself; I didn't want the gardener somehow calling up and ingesting pieces of my mom and dad, their heavy history. And as I shut the lid on all of it, I thought about how I had never liked those sweets.

I bent over and picked Fluffy up from his patch of sunlight there on the grass, walked into the house and inspected its nearly empty insides and knew I would have to move some day soon. Me and the cat.

We sat in one of the few remaining chairs and I began with him again, my hand working at that old cat's mattes briskly now, for hours and hours, almost nonstop.

By the time I felt like moving on, Fluffy's fur had acquired an incredible shine; in higher spirits myself, I picked up all that paperwork again, and, of course, I began to talk to him about having a DNA analysis run. I've always thought him a very rational, a very scientific, cat. How else to verify this detective's facts? And then I thought about how Fluffy had been there. Fluffy was privy to all that had happened in the past. Do you remember Manuel? I asked the cat, who just stared with suddenly slightly cinched and very creepy yellow eyes. Surely angry at my asking for his help after having abandoned him as I had. Have I said that, among other things, he seems to be a spiteful cat? So I considered DNA again, alone, before I decided I would be able to see it; I would be able to trust my own eyes. A brother. I would be able to trust in that.

And then I began to imagine him. A brother. Manolo the cobbler. Manolo, no relation to the shoe man rich ladies love, but Manolo, the last remaining relation of mine.

I went to the bathroom and pulled my long hair away from my face, to see what I would look like as a man, and as I stared at the he me in the mirror I knew that the real he would be able to tell me things, describe a smell, the fall of light upon her head, fingers as they worked a pen, the way that her lips parted when she pulled a glass up to them. And though I had now begun to admit that at some level this is what had made it impossible to actually look for him before, had terrified me, I was sure now that I wanted it. I wanted to know all of those minute things he knew. A mother no longer just an idea on which my fears could attach but all the little details of her person too. I opened the medicine cabinet which I had forgotten to clean out when I'd emptied the rest of the house and saw all of the same containers I had seen in there before, except, of course, the nail polish. There was the plastic bottle of alcohol, the blood pressure medication, the shaving cream, the box of face powder. I pulled it out and poured the circular receptacle of loose powder into my hand from out of the red and black box. *Gitana*: gypsy. I lifted the top of the container and took out the big puff, closed the cabinet door and then layered and layered that powder in front of the mirror, a thick beige coat. Hello, Manuel, I am your mother, I said, stared at myself, and blinked quick my eyes.

I wrote him at the address the detective had provided. A letter re-written and torn up many many times, until I decided on the simplest one: I am your long lost sister. Did you know you had one? A twin. And now it is twin time. Love, Mona. And then I gave him my addresses, both kinds. And again, a week later, my heart stopped, and started and I breathed out my hundredth loud cartoon gasp when I saw the heading in my inbox: sibling search successful: twin time. Of course, you are the older one, the text read. The wily and responsible one. The courageous searching one. The lost brother finding one. Call me and we can meet and I promise to bring you a pair of red shoes.

I felt such a coward, a liar and fake, yet in his e-mail he had called me courageous. So with my heavy suitcase, father packed tight inside between two almost identical black sweaters, I flew to New York the next week.

The first visit

I t took place in a dream three days before I actually met him. He came to me and even I was surprised by how much his face was mine. Most twins will tell you they don't see it, the differences are what stand out, but to me he and I seemed one. I've always been here, he said without speaking; I know, I replied.

He laid down close to me, his head right next to mine and my skin burned like a fever first and then tingled warm for a long time. I lifted my eyes a bit, sleep heavy, moved them measured about the room. It was all the same, everything in place, my computer on the bamboo desk, the window above it, Fluffy asleep on the box at our feet. The box was different.

My breath came slow and deep. I didn't remember a trunk in my room, there at the foot of the bed. I brought it, he said, again without speaking. I looked over at him and as I gazed into his eyes I recalled the dream I'd been having when he arrived to wake me. I was in an apartment, I said, which was not familiar; my father there too, as a young man. He had big soft eyes, I went on, though they would not meet mine. I didn't force him to take me in for I understood that he was my father before me, before the heaviness of being had set itself deep into his life. I walked away from him where he lay and made my way down a long hall, cautiously opened a door I found to the right. I stepped hesitantly in, and focused on the box I'd just seen Fluffy lying on top of (and I now wondered if Manuel had in fact brought it into my room how he'd gotten it there from inside this dream). I looked around then, and my heart lifted; it was a generous and large space, with a beautiful bed right in the center. Excited I thought to rush back to my father, tell him this was where he should lay, but my legs failed me and in my struggle to make them move my eye was caught by a huge spider on the wooden rafters; I then noticed there were hundreds of tiny ones, just hatched, coming down on lengthening webs. My breath stopped as the dread spread inside me and still I could not move. And then somehow I did, I made my way to him with heavy dragging limbs, each step an immense effort, and attempted to yell, scream at him for help, but my voice stuck inside me and though I tried and tried it would not come. In a full panic now, I raised my heavy arm to his and saw his face was now without features: he had lost his eyes and mouth and nose, and still I pulled him, voicelessly yanking him toward the door. When we made it to the room I saw those hundreds of tiny spiders just hanging there, patient, and then that giant one, as big as my father's back, cream colored, now sitting on that box, and I wanted him to kill it but could still not say a thing. As I looked about for a tool it jumped onto his shoulders and we both ran my voice finally coming a long scream carrying us down the hall and toward the front door. I wanted to pull it off of his back—he was stumbling ahead of me, guiding himself with searching outstretched hands since without eyes he could not see—but I could not find the strength; and then I saw it lodge itself deep into him like a tick and I felt sick that I could not bring myself to yank it off. My weakness, inability to move or speak or help, would kill him, I knew. We never made it to the front door.

I felt my breath catching and looked over at Manuel where he lay next to me; he fixed his eyes on mine, You live in a haunted house, Mona, our mother, the ghost. It was the first time either one of us had spoken out loud and I was startled by his voice, the soft English accent.

Yes, I answered.

I'm here now, he said.

I know.

One last thing.

Yes?

The baker was not our father.

On waking

shook my head as if to free myself of the dream, though I could not shake Manuel. I knew he'd been there, was still there somehow. Though the red box was gone now and Fluffy lay curled as he always did on the bed down at my feet.

Of course I had thought this before, that my father was not my father, though I'm unsure of how or why it had come to me on the few occasions that it had been a clear thought. And it's true too that though I had thought it I'd deny it to myself right away, for if he were not mine, whom did I have?

But how can I tell you all this?

I do remember him welling-up once. Though I'm confused about what happened that time, what got the ball rolling. I'd done something, of that we can be sure, it hadn't just come out of nowhere and he would never have initiated anything like that; so maybe it was when he found out I'd attacked that girl for mentioning my mother, for speaking of her in front of those two guys. This makes sense, for it was probably just a day or two after I'd rushed home and questioned him about her death the way I had, so that when he got the phone call from the school about what I'd done to that girl he must have been already shaken in regard to me and my mom and that has to be why he came in kind of dazed and then looked straight at me the way that he did, deep into my eyes for the first time in my life, and just when

I thought he might finally say something that felt actual and real, he apologized. "I'm sorry," he said. And then he said something like, "I haven't done right by your mother." It was so strange. The gravity in his tone. A man making amends. He was so sad as he said it all, and I knew then that at the center of his words he was saying that he was not my father. And though he'd barely whispered it, his hands began shaking in that way that he had; I was frightened by what I'd just thought, what I'd heard embedded in his statement, and didn't know what to do with it, pulled back slowly, inched away from his shaking hands there in our living room and then I pretended I had not heard it there at the edges and he never repeated anything like it again. I probably went out and got drunk with Mineko that night. We probably met up with some slightly older guys whom we let fondle and touch in ways we weren't quite ready for as we stared straight into black night. And then my father and I went back to our before that statement and everything it carried in it way of barely skimming the surface of reality. And I had been successful at forgetting it all. It had become some deep neglected memory, lying asleep in some swamp. Until Manuel. His showing up in my dream with that box.

And my mother. When that girl said it, in the instant before I leapt on her with bared claws, what she said seemed so real. It rang true. My mom told me your mom just dumped you, took off with her hairdresser and left you behind sounded true. And if, as I've heard told, the devil is that one who at the crossroads takes you off your direct path… makes you take on other options, steers you clear of safe known roads, then my devil had been twelve years old, a red-mawed long limbed loose lipped pubescent fiend that went by the name Angie.

Of course you hear things, know them. You hear things and maybe even deeply know that they are real. But you forget them. You have to live your life, the day to day of it, and so you forget these horrible things you think, or hear. Take the other version, even if it doesn't ever seem quite right, create a better, less problematic place from which to live, from which to move, and eat and sleep, for if you don't then you will stand, staring blind, paralyzed until you starve immobile in that one spot, sink into yourself and die.

And then again, maybe there are lots of different ways to know the world, your place in it. Maybe the stories and dreams and make-believe help us with our facts. Maybe we all move between these different ways of knowing every day, constantly, within the measure of an instant sometimes: from dream to metaphor to myth to story, and verifiable fact, and all the other tools which we can muster together to help us stay alive.

Someone like me

I sat waiting in the coffeeshop where we'd agreed to meet and Manuel came and I wanted to please him and I wanted him to love me and so I didn't talk. What could I say? Hello. I am Mona and I grew up on a hill in Podunk, California with my now dead depressed baker of a father. And, you should know, I was raised on the lies he fed me, the biggest one of which was that our mother died in childbirth, and I never but once questioned him though from a very early age I had my doubts. And, by the way, you were never mentioned so it's like you were dead too, or at least like you were never born. I could then shake his hand and add: You see, I'm a coward and so though things didn't seem to add up, never seemed right, I just took it, and made up a bunch of firmly sealed stories myself which very closely matched all his (and which someone like you might feel the need to call lies) to force it all into making sense, and in this way I never had to stand up to his falsehoods and face the fact that you had left.

Then I could offer to buy him a coffee, defer going any further, and ask him to tell me about his life instead.

He did tell me about his life, but, of course, it didn't go quite like that. I saw and knew him through the large plate-glass window as he walked up, approached the front door and, cigarette in hand, took one last drag. There he was, exactly as in my dream—his olive skin, great big dark eyes, disheveled brown hair, alike and not alike for though he hunched he was much taller than I. And as he'd made his way into the coffee shop, overladen by his outsize shoulder bag (the same red as the box he'd brought into my dream), I was horrified by the thought that he was someone I could easily have made-out with in a bar. Or I could have passed him on the street, of course not known who he was, found him attractive, gone home and fantasized. My hands were shaking, then, I was so nervous, and it was easier to see him like that. Distant. Not mine. A faraway somebody. A handsome man in line at a coffee shop. Those huge deep-set eyes. And yet, what if Manuel and I had unwittingly ended up in bed together? Had neither my mother nor father ever thought about that? A dangerous situation, given the consequences—we've all read of sixth fingers, human tails—for look at the way that he smiled at the other people in line, shifted on his feet and thoughtfully looked down a lot. How could they not have even considered the possibility of that?

But now he was my brother. And soon he would know I was his sister.

When he turned to look over at me there at my table from where he stood up near that counter my heart raced and I could feel my ears burning. His eyes registered surprise, then he smiled over, almost walked away from the counter, but then raised his eyebrows and pointed with his beautiful hand to indicate that he had just to wait one more moment, finally got his coffee and then came and gave me a long kiss on the cheek, his hand gently taking hold of the opposite side of my head, drawing me near; when after many long moments he pulled back I could see he had tears in his eyes. And immediately I was jealous, for I wanted to be the one crying, I wanted to be the beautiful one who smiled in a way that made another heart melt, but in the moment I thought all this, in an almost simultaneous set of motions he wiped at those eyes and handed me a box, so that I was instantly ashamed of my jealousy and self-conscious too about not having brought anything for him except my father, that dubious gift; and now the horridness of my selfishness took over, for a moment, until his shifting eyes reminded me to lift the top of the box and I saw that inside there was a pair of lollipop red wedges, and he had not even asked me my size. And of course he'd gotten it right: 6 1/2.

I'm Mona, I said.

I know, he answered, grabbing hold of my shifting eyes.

I glanced at the shoes again, Thank you, I whispered, overwhelmed by his entrance. And by my stupid overarching attention to each minute fluctuation of my own emotions, to the point of not being able to concentrate on another human being. On my brother.

You're very welcome. They're a bit Terry de Havilland, a bit Dorothy as slut. I hope they're not too much, he whispered in return.

Oh, no. I don't know who that Terry person is but they're the nicest shoes I've ever had. I'll never take them off, I said, wiping a tear from my cheek.

You okay? he asked. I looked up at him, and we stared into each other's eyes: and I saw myself then, tiny but complete, reflected inside my brother's big brown eyes.

He settled himself down at my side and took it up, the talk, and I was grateful that I didn't have to speak, a lump of bare emotion, taking in his presence, this brother who was and was not mine; my outline fell away, all just nervous energy now, and he moved right into it, taking over and re-forming me with his easy chat, as though this were the most casual meeting in the world, the two of us.

Manuel

He grew up in London, the never legally adopted son of a tousled blonde hairdresser and his petite and beautiful never legally sanctioned Mexican wife (My mother!). He said his dad was still, at nearly sixty, a cad. As a result he'd suffered a tumultuous childhood, his mother and father a drunk and squabbling shambles much of the time. Though as a small child he'd happily stepped into the space their fighting made for him, for those fights meant his mother would take him into her room, just the two of them. Tell him things he was not to reveal to Michael, or anybody else, delicious and special and just for him. Her every word a secret pact.

She'd shut the door behind them and they'd lay in bed and the telling would start, their fingers intermingling and caressing as she told her private tales. He had a sister, she whispered. She was a twin. Her name was Mona and she had his own big eyes. Like a foundling she'd been left with a very kindly baker soon after their birth. Though for a while they had all lived together—a make-believe family—in a tiny house with this man of sugary treats; for only a short while however, a month or two or six. And now she sometimes thought that they could have stayed like that forever, in that in-between place, should have found a way to stay. They could have made a slow molasses dream world inside the baker's life. Though she did not love him she could have calmed her inner struggle, learned that thick syrup slow-pace pour and they could have lived just fine. Like a princess in some fairy tale she could have sacrificed. Hindsight, they say.

Impossible anyway, for a spell had been cast upon her and her mind and her heart had raced to terrifying places—valleys of disappearance where dragons ate daily at your insides—and she'd had to run; it was urgent and there could be no second thought. The catch: she could only bring one to London… someday she would explain, put together the puzzle, decipher riddles, help him understand. She had chosen him, for a boy seemed somehow more suited for that long and unknown voyage, the vicissitudes and trials…

When he looked at her with both triumph and terror in his eyes she continued in a more serious lower-toned hush:

But one day very soon, together, when things had really settled down, just the two of them—now, it had to be when everything was just right—would make the long trip back and retrieve his left behind sister. She worked on this plan every day, he must understand, drew up maps and diagrams which she then burned or threw out so as not to get caught, and then kept it all ordered deep inside her own head. She had money stashed away; she would show him sometime. But for now he must understand this was A SECRET.

She was very nearly on him now, staring into his eyes: he was not to tell anyone any of it, ever, not anyone. And taking seriously the importance of her trust, bound by her weighty confidence, tales for only him, he had not. Until now.

Sometimes, depending on her mood, she would put a dress on him. She would call him Mona and teach him how to dance, his arms held in an arc high above his head, toes pointed, legs in a straight line. That's right! she would clap her hands and joyfully exclaim. He could make her laugh like this and then he'd rush over to her, confused and embarrassed by his own act, and she'd cover him in kisses. She was so pretty, his mother. She'd rub and caress his fingers, move to his belly and his hair and his arms and begin to again whisper stories quiet in his ear.

Of course he would never think to share with Michael. This was their special game and Mona was only for them.

But, there was always something else, for deep within him there was a constant black electric fear, a deep low level thing, a humming perhaps he would call it, which was fed by the possibility that another spell could be cast upon her and that she would have to leave again... this time it would be him...

So though their game was mostly delicious—she needed him so deeply, so intensely, so very very much—depending on the amount of truth he thought there was in it all at any given time, there was also a varying degree of terror at the center. As a result he would always behave, perfect boy, be what she needed of him, follow, let her lead, and never ask for any more than he could get. For Mama, he knew, could very well one day simply be not there.

As an adolescent these games had long been over when he began to take refuge from his parents' fighting alone in cloistered bedroom hunched before a large sketchpad. A couple of times during these years he'd been bold enough to ask about his father, for from the beginning they had been clear that Michael was not his real dad. She wouldn't reply, would completely ignore him and go on with her dusting, or magazine browsing, or cigarette smoking as if it were an all-consuming task, something to which she must be fully applied. One time, brave, he dared to bring up the baker, Is it him? Is he the one? he asked; though he somehow knew he should not push and mention Mona. These two beings from those earlier times, from inside his childhood games, he had always strongly felt were only hers to bring forth; it was unspoken, but they belonged to her and she was the one who decided when and where to share and so he was stretching it with the baker; he had to be careful and measured... though he was no longer a small boy there was still that fear in his middle... that humming... a blackness into which he could fall forever... into which he could step and then descend

descend

descend...

She looked at him distracted and his heart stopped, The baker? she asked back, as if confused he even knew that he existed. No, it was not him, she firmly added. And then her mood shifted, she walked over and took on the voice of his childhood, hushed and covert; it was then she told him of the writer. She whispered her love of him, described his curls and his slow talk, and then how one day, before even she knew she was pregnant, he suddenly left. To finish his studies in France. He must have been too moved to say good-bye when he went, he loved me so much, she said, though her voice had shifted once again and came out hard. She began to cry, tried to go on but could not. And he sat motionless, though he averted his eyes. The baker had helped her at that time, she told when she collected herself, her tone softening again. He had taken her in.

And for years she had thought she might find the writer, though she was so anxious, lost, continually dazed. She barely knew where she was. And after the facts of her life, after she and Michael seemed to settle down, she never even thought to try.

She looked away and that was the end. She had nothing left to say.

He brought up the writer again, two more times, but the first time she said she had already talked to him all about it and would not do so again, and the second time she refused even to raise her head. When he pressed her she looked over from inside her romance novel, really angry with him for the first time in her life, and demanded that he stop.

He never got a name.

One day, a few months later, he rifled through all of Michael's wigs until he found one with long, dark hair, short straight bangs. He wasn't sure now why he'd done it, though at the time there'd been no question. He went into his mother's room and put it on, adjusted and added a little paisley dress, laid himself down on the bed facing away from the door and waited until he heard the approach of his mother's footsteps. His breathing quickened and then he heard her stop short. He turned his face slowly and in an altered voice said, Hi Mama, do you remember me? She faltered and then began to weep. He was shocked, overcome and ashamed, and perplexed all at once and he could not strip it all off—hair and dress—and rush to her like a part of him wanted, was paralyzed so that he could not move at all until she ran from out of the doorway.

The old games seemed too much for him then, could so easily take over and horrify in a way he'd intimated into their margins, their terrifying edge. It was so much easier to not think about the baker or the father or the sister, for it was too tumultuous, confused and muddled and indeterminate; and his mother, he had to wonder at her awful depths, question how he could go on loving her so completely when she was not only the one who had been left pregnant, but also the one who had done the unspeakable leaving; his sister.

And something else…

How do you go on living guilt-free when you are the one who was chosen? How do you pretend it was not you too who left, who was one day simply suddenly not there?

The three of them

His exotic looks were now an asset, no longer just the fuel for the ridicule of his childhood and with the help of his dad he made his way to the fringes of the fashion world where he, quiet and diligent, worked his way up to become a young shoe designer for Patrick C.

Shoes are made for walking and his mother was always walking, he said. Away. Leaving Michael again and again. He remembered himself a tiny boy in her arms being held, hanging heavy his head, looking down, noticing her shoes—square heeled silver sandals with leather cutouts, little circles dangling playful at the top—the beauty in them.

As he got older he realized that he'd always worried that she should look good in her walking away, like a movie star, Alida Valli in *The Third Man* when she walks right past Joseph Cotton, sure of herself, that strong step an image of everything she holds inside. Or like Rita Tushingham in *The Knack and How to Get It*. Those shoes. The once dim girl now leaving the sarcastic men behind, in control at the end.

From his youngest days they'd spent a lot of time together in the low light of the cinema, he and his mother. At revival houses mostly where they'd watch Cocteau fairy tales, Fellini and Godard whom he (and he suspected she too) watched mostly for the fashion; the American films from the 40s, staring up at all of those strong women, Barbara Stanwyck and Katherine Hepburn and Claudette Colbert, and while lost in the beauty on the screen, or in the minutes just after they walked out they imagined together that she was one of them, tough and smart and strong, although soon they had to admit that she wasn't anything like them at all. For the way that it always ended in the film that was their life was with the heroine defeated, returning to Michael yet again, and with him, pitiable sidekick, small and weak, an insignificance trailing on hesitant shuffling feet behind.

But there had to have been much more in her leaving and then going back to Michael, things he didn't understand, would never understand. He had been so angry with her for it as a child but now, as an adult, he thought of his friends, how many he had that did the same thing. Leave and go back. Go back and leave. He'd done it himself with more than one person. Though, of course, to a child it all seems so horrible. Devastating each time. And yet she always went back.

Michael was constantly cheating on her. And—he'd thought about this—he supposed this cheating actually provided her with the reason for her tears and her anger. What he meant to say was that he made it easier for her to feel things she had perhaps always already felt, or to outwardly express things she forever continually carried inside. That may partially be why she always returned to him. He gave her a way back into those feelings again without having them take over from inside.

Though he also made her laugh. And there was something animal in them. It had embarrassed him as a child. None of his friends' parents groped and kissed like that...

He stopped short, as if made uncomfortable again by his memories of them together, turned and reached over and into his red bag and began to pull out the photographs. And with those pictures he continued to tell the story of their lives:

I thought you might want to see these. A lot of them are in books now. Michael was a stylist and got prints of much of what was shot for his portfolio. Look, here's our mother.

And there she was, dancing with some man, doing the twist perhaps, her hair shoulder length and spinning around her face so that you couldn't see her features at all, her sleeveless beige shift dress and matching square-toed low heeled shoes. Beyond the limits of her clothes, though you could not see her face, you saw a lot of arm, both of them, and a good portion of leg, again, both, and a bit of the side of her neck. He told me the picture was reproduced in a David Bailey book with a caption that read: couple dancing. I wondered at the hundreds, thousands, maybe millions of people who had seen my mother in that photograph, and not known who she was, not known that she was my mom, that she was Mara who had left her daughter and run off to London with her son while her daughter and this girl's stand-in father pretended she was dead, the father making up stories about the dead mother, the daughter never but once asking any questions, never really wanting to unearth even one terrifying fact, while he, this man who had once loved her baked cakes in California for all the other people's happy lives. Had anyone ever looked at that picture and even come close to guessing at any of that?

I'll show you the book when you come to my flat, he said. That's not Michael, by the way. Michael's better looking, and here he paused for nearly a minute while he stared at our mom. She was probably trying to get back at him for something that night, he continued. He gave her the best haircuts though, don't you think? and look at those shoes; they're Courreges. He got a lot of free stuff from the designers he styled for. And here, with my mother on the table in front of me, the focus of his attention on her hair and her shoes, Michael's good looks, turned my stomach a bit.

Michael was a bastard to our mother, he went on, but I have to say that he helped me quite a lot when I began. And he never made fun of me for sitting in my room and drawing all day, the way some-one else's dad might have. Never once told me to go outside. What I mean is that he isn't all bad, you know; and he never made me feel like I didn't belong to him, never ever used that.

I reached over and touched his arm with my fingertip, felt his skin, and Manuel finally put that picture down. He picked up another, this one of a blond girl in a bikini standing atop a table in a dark pub, Look, here's Jill Kennington, he said. He did her hair for this shot.

And like this he flipped through nearly two dozen pictures, narrating stories from his early life. He'd thrown up on Jean Shrimpton, just hours before that picture of her and Dudley Moore dancing was shot. She was inhumanly gorgeous and she had held him and while she bounced him up and down on her lap he'd thrown up all over the dress she was supposed to wear for the shoot. And she'd just laughed. She hadn't thrown some kind of pretty girl tantrum or screamed or dropped him. She'd just taken a hit off of Michael's joint, and laughed, before she handed him off to our mom. Manuel had met all these models, who now stared out at me, immortalized, looking so fluid and in high contrast standing next to rigid statues or nearly naked atop pub tables surrounded by factory workers in that falling London light. But, out of all this was I supposed to be getting some sense of our mom? Where was she in all of that? A kid sitting in some corner watching, waiting for her baby to be handed back? There was one picture of Michael and in it Vidal Sassoon has an arm around his shoulder and they are laughing big, looking deep through the camera and into our eyes. Vidal Sassoon, looking so formal in his little black suit, had once cut four year old Manuel's hair. This was after he had given Mia Farrow her five thousand dollar haircut, he said.

But what about my mother? I wanted to ask. Where was she in all of this? and I was feeling jealous that he had gotten this still shadow of a mother, this outline of a mom, who was now really dead and I would never ever know; and I'd been stuck driving cakes and tarts around with my dejected father while he had been living this incredibly full of beautiful shoes and gorgeous women and expensive haircuts and groovy pass-the-joint wonderful life.

I saw that he was growing upset too, was flipping back through the pictures and once again had the shot of Jill Kennington in his hands. He fucked her that same night, he said, That was the worst. He would brag about the women he'd bang. He looked away, put the picture down and then began ordering and then stashing them all back in his big bag while I began to wonder if this had indeed all been brought for me or if he carried his history around with him like this, weighing him down on one side, all of the time.

And then he said, Mara died almost exactly a year ago, by the way.

The letters

Though I'm not sure why it seemed important just then I asked him what day and when he told me I immediately realized my father had died just two weeks after she had, and my heart grew heavier still. Their lives seemed so tied together, even though they had lived them so very far apart.

And for just a few faint and confused moments, I see a teenaged Manuel, hair short, messy jeans and scuffed up Vans, and he is in our kitchen with my father and they lean in to each other, talking serious, and my father is kind and patient, teaching him how to do something as Manuel nods, a pile of little mushrooms in his outstretched hand. And I see my mother too. I see her looking lovely in the short paisley dress Manuel described wearing when he pretended to be me, and she smiles openly as my father walks into the room and sets the table before her.

And then I leave that world of never to be possibility and focus on him there before me, think of getting the letter my father sent and handing it over to him, then pulling my father out too, introducing the two, but before I can get at any of it he pulls out a big envelope from inside his bag, Look, this is for you, he says.

I take it and immediately notice it is a letter as well and my head spins.

I have one for you too, I manage to say, baffled, confused. And then after a minute I say, From my father, and then I give him his and he looks at it and I look at mine more closely and I see how crumpled it is. And I see that it is from my mother and then I see that he has already read my long letter! He hasn't even tried to tape it back shut. Did you read this? What is wrong with you? I yell. Here I've been thinking you were so perfect for the last hour and a half! I never even thought of opening yours!

Now come on, nobody's perfect, he says, to which I roll my eyes. Sorry, he adds more sincerely. And then, You know, I really do think you're the older one. You're kind of uptight.

And I have to admit that I am a bit relieved each time I notice some flaw in Manuel... I want to magnify it and make it vast so that there can be some space for me, somewhere where I can fit—with all of my monstrosities and shortcomings and imperfections and failings—fit and feel right.

We now have our rightful letters and we decide to read them together... though he has already partially cheated the significance of this act.

And in her letter to me she says a few things about Mexico City, and these things she says make me want to be there with her and then she tells about the writer who moved away. She tells me about Michael and how he appeared in her life like a dream, to save her from her own reality. Because, she tells, before the fact of him she thought she would go mad. She talks about my father, his kindness and her inability to contain what was inside at that time. She doesn't say anything about me except I am sorry. And though I am crying this makes me angry for it isn't enough. I go back to the part about my father, Eduardo, the baker, the only one I ever had and she tells me of his gentleness, his patience, his big heart. I know these things, I say out loud. And then again all she can do is apologize.

And there are no firm facts about the writer. It is a half letter, a half-hearted confession; it is the only thing I have ever gotten from her in my life and there is no resolution. There are just as many questions with answers Manuel and I will never be able to find.

My father's letter opens: Dear Son, he then tries to pretend he is our dad, talks about us as babies, talks about his love of our mom. Then four pages down he admits it. Apologizes and I can just imagine the tears in his eyes as he writes it, I'm sorry. He tells Manuel how much he loved him, that when they left a big part of him died.

I want to crush up both letters, burn them, throw them in the trash. But Manuel takes them, smooths them out, and I am glad, just then, that he is at my side.

Manuel, I say when I've settled, I brought something else.

He looks at me and I can see that he is both confused by my grave tone and expectant too. I bend down into my satchel and pull out the large Ziploc bag; I turn it so that he can see my father's name scrawled on the front. I wanted you two to meet, I tell him.

Okay, he answers. And his voice is kind and not mocking. Hello there, he says to my father.

He then picks him up and places him in his bag along with those pictures, Let's go to my flat, he says, wiping my soggy cheek with his beautiful hand.

Yes, I answer, wringing out the tears from around my neckline. We wipe up the table with a handful of napkins and walk through the Lower East Side to Chinatown and 84 Eldridge Street, up the five impossibly narrow and stench filled flights of stairs and into his one room apartment where we lock ourselves in for four days, laying in his double bed barely breathing, side by twin side.

Two beginnings

J ust before falling asleep, exhausted both, he told me how she'd died in a car accident. Weeping, Manuel said, after fighting with Michael again (and still) after so many years she ran out of the house and was hit by a taxi as she crossed High Street. The driver said she ran into the street without looking, appeared from out of nowhere, almost like she leapt into him. She must have been back in Mexico City, I thought, in the midst of those tears and so forgot to look right.

She seemed to know it was coming, Manuel said, his voice cold and flat now, because just a day or so before she told me that if anything were ever to happen to her I had to give you that letter. I was confused because though at some level I truly believed you were real there was a strange and dreamlike and from inside her mind quality about you; so that when she showed me where it sat in her dresser, an actual letter addressed to an actual you, I could do nothing but nod. And then that taxi hitting her just one or two days later. It was so strange. I've never said this before, only allowed myself to think it once or twice, but it was like she wanted it, like she had it planned out, Mona. And then the way the driver said she ran into the street... at precisely the wrong moment? It's all so odd.

We were both silent for a long while, and I thought about my mother then, the way she'd died, her blind rushing into the streets, and how often this happens to me, no world outside for the weight of what's inside. I don't know Manuel, I said. I can get that lost inside myself. Perhaps, he said. And then we tried to shut our eyes.

And then I was sure I'd never sleep, except I must have for the next thing I knew I was waking from a strange dream in which I saw my mother screaming, crying: her face was distorted and her cries came from inside; from deep down deep inside, from Mexico City and her mother, and the man who was our father, and California, and my father, and me left there, behind. And then I saw Michael was there too; he sat across the room in a big red armchair and though I now realized it was him she was directing her cries at he seemed so passive he was barely there at all; except I noticed a slight and insolent smile play upon his lips. And then she flew at him and he remained emotionless as he unflinchingly grabbed at her tiny feeble woman hands when she lunged herself, beating upon his chest. His face shifted, began to show some anger then, as she screamed that he must listen. He had to listen. And after a strange silence, a couple of minutes of him just holding her firm by the wrists, her sobbing started up again and through the words between these cries I began to decipher that he'd slept with another one. And then she stopped trying to beat on him and doubled over, begging him for compassion, begging him to listen, falling on the floor as she whimpered that he had to at least show a bit of sympathy and not flaunt it in such ways; she understood, she said; she did, could put up with it, he knew, he must have known, if he just didn't show it off like that, his hand upon that knee, right in front of her, in front of everyone. And then her voice became a whisper as she said that they were always so different from her, so tall and so blond and this made her think that he hated her even more, and she began to cry, softly now. And it was then that I noticed Manuel, Manuel, a small child, a pretty little boy crouching in the corner and now that it seemed safe, now that she seemed safe, he ran to her and grasped her waist, before she was up, pulling away from his small hands, and again throwing herself against his dad. Michael's own hand went up toward her face as he yelled at her that she was the one who should show some compassion and just shut up. Stop. Her hysteria was too much. He couldn't go on.

How often had that hand come down upon her face?

And then I saw her again, and she was different. Her expression steely and determined and my heart soared a little and I was proud of her; it was a moment of her leaving, and she was commanding as she stooped to pick Manuel up from where he squatted on the floor, from where he was squatted over playing with a little toy car, making the noises of a horn, a beep beep beep, and then she swooped him into her arms and was leaving, with the small boy, the tiny boy, looking down, focusing on an object beyond her arms around his waist, for objects are safe and emotionless. Objects aren't volatile; shoes know how to run away. Manuel, a tiny little man now, was serious, telling himself he wasn't scared, focusing on the craftsmanship of leather, on the pretty rhinestone buckle, on the playful chunky heel.

And then a week later they lay laughing, all it took was a cliché, a dozen dark red roses, and there she was and there Michael was and they were laughing, draped across a long couch, a glass of whiskey in each of their hands.

Mother weeping, flailing, one day. And then kissing, open and inviting on the next. And it was my mother that I had until then wanted to see, but it was little Manuel that I presently focused on; in the midst of their tornado of emotion, of their playing out of dumb roles, it was he that I wanted to look at more. It was he that I wanted to now see.

We woke up in the same moment. And we were holding hands. At some point in the dark night we must have reached out for each other. And in those first wakeful moments, those most confused yet lucid moments of the whole day, I knew that I had always known about Manuel. That I had always felt him, and his absence. That every breath I exhaled carried something of him in it. I missed you, I said inside my own head.

Are you awake? he asked.

I just woke up, I answered.

Me too, he said. Mona, what are we going to do now?

I don't know. And for minutes and minutes there was only our mingled breathing and the silence beyond it, unbroken, in that old tenement apartment with its ugly yellowed walls. He should paint it, I thought, before I went on: As soon as my father told me about you things started to unravel for me. Not that they'd been perfectly raveled before. But I do think I've always known about you, remembered you somehow. I understand though what it means to not look. To be frightened of what you will find. I turned away from the ceiling and toward him, into his eyes, Manuel, why do you think she left me?

I don't know, Mona. I'm so very sorry. Though I don't think there's anything I can possibly say to help either one of us understand.

He drew his heavy gaze away from me and back up at the ceiling, Some things just don't make any sense, but maybe we can look for something in those letters, some feeling, an air of something. We lay without speaking again for a long time.

Did I tell you I once almost killed a girl?

You almost killed a girl?

Yeah. Well. I pulled her hair real hard. Manuel laughed. No, *real* hard. I laughed too now, I had clumps of it left in my hands when they pulled me off of her. She'd said something about my mother running off with a man. In front of two guys. I liked one of them… I mean it was a huge crush. And in the end she was right. I don't know, Manuel, I said crying now, I think you're wrong about her too. I have to believe that she did not kill herself. I have to believe that she was going to come find me. Horrible accidents do happen, you know. Just like that. And I think she was going to come. Maybe she was even on her way to find me when she died.

Okay, he said.

I think I have to go home for a while. I think I need some time to sort everything out. Can I take your letter with me? I promise to send it back.

You can bring it back, you know, he tugged at my hair a little bit. And then he added, Mona, what are we going to do with your dad?

I don't know. Can we talk about that later? Do you wanna go for a walk? Go out? Maybe find some food.

And with that we left the depths of his apartment's sickeningly yellow insides.

The streets of New York

We wandered around for hours, not speaking, like each other's silent shadows. And on Grand Street the scent from the weeks old fish guts in the stopped-up municipally ignored gutters in front of the Chinese markets flew up at us strong and confrontational from out of that fuming ground. Fruit and vegetables sat piled on make-shift stands in bunches of just recognizable colors and silhouettes, and behind and above these fruit stands bright orange Peking ducks hung strangely beautiful and heady and intense. The throngs of people, pushing and knocking into us pulled us along like somnambulant fish so that any pausing to make things out lasted only a second and soon Manuel and I were holding our arms out a bit from our sides like we saw the old women do to keep from getting thrashed any further by that oblivious hurried mass, he moving slightly ahead of me before looking back to spot me and then stopping to gaze in a storefront at medicinal herbs and animal parts in fancy red and gold boxes. I moved ahead of him and made my way toward three wooden barrels full of tofu sitting outside a tiny store inside of which two women fried and packaged further kinds of soy. Manuel grabbed my hand suddenly and pulled me out of that pause and back into the flow for just one second before leading me toward what looked like a little plant store in front of which sat an ancient Chinese man, who smiled and nodded as we walked inside. And then, in the dim misty light we began to make out hundreds of elaborate bird cages in all sizes, tiny and delicate little sculptures holding single tweeting finches to large impressive reproductions of temples full of flitting parakeets, yellows and greens and oranges in an elaborate flap dance, and then parrots in ones and twos who called out to each other from their enclosures across that big room and lovebirds who sat close together in standard sized cages and beautiful pink-hued cockatoos who perched alone and poised, all of them surrounded by orchids and ferns and palms and bromeliads and other tropical shade-giving plants. We wandered and found a large gold temple in the far corner of that room and inside this temple stood a big toucan, still and stunning and lonely, and we rested next to him looking through that huge room for what seemed like an hour and then I shut my eyes and listened to all the calls and flapping of wings. And when we finally walked outside I noticed we were holding hands again and wondered how long we'd been doing so as we'd listened to those birds, too awed to notice our fingers intertwined.

The sun falling now, Manuel and I kept walking and looking in windows and pulling at each other's arms through the streets of lower Manhattan, until it turned dark and we could peer deep inside the living spaces of Soho and Tribeca, wondering, like our mother had once done alone on the streets of Mexico City, how it was that people got those magical lives.

A twin, after all

As it turned out, Manuel had been in the woods just like me; in fact, as a result he'd lost his shoe designer slot at P.C.; that's why he'd moved to New York from London. He got this cheap sublet from an artist friend who was crazy but rich and had built himself a new loft, and Manuel had been living off his savings and the good graces of his friends until recently when he went back to making shoes in collaboration with two girls who made dresses and sold them out of the back of a laundromat on the Lower East Side, two blocks from the coffeeshop where we'd first met.

It's better this way. I found a good cheap fabricator in Brazil. And I'd really rather not work for someone else. It's more fun to try to start something up.

I'm glad you're feeling better, I said.

I tried to write a bit, he said shyly, you know, to make some sense of the last year. I thought, if our father was a writer, then there was a chance some of it had flowed through. And he went over to a make-shift desk and flipped through a pile of papers that he ordered then stuck in an envelope. He walked over and handed the package to me, I was wrong; I'm no writer and went back to making shoes instead.

We agreed that I could take his pages, and both letters and see what I could do with it all.

Late that night we took my father and a shovel Manuel had borrowed from one of his artist friends and jumped in a cab to the cloisters in the upper reaches of Fort Tyron Park. I read a plaque commemorating the first American woman soldier, Margaret Corbin, and thought of myself as a warrior too, fierce in my Dorothy as slut shoes while I took turns digging along with Manuel. We buried my father there, freed him of his plastic bag so he could mix freely with the soil that looked out on the Hudson ... far away from California and the sadness to which in his life he had been so bound.

The next morning we took another taxi together, this time to JFK, and before I stepped through security I hugged Manuel tight around his neck...

The flight

On the plane home I pulled his writing out of the envelope and this is how it began:

The Dead Mother

This is not the first time, she said. When I lived with the baker. I wanted to be a plant. That time, a tree. I wanted to be a tree. To dig my feet in the dark earth and take the sun right in. I stopped eating then too. But began again because you were inside. It all turned when I heard your hearts.

She was in bed as she said all this, her voice heavy and thick and slow. She was sick in ways I could now see so I locked the door and kept the key and I wouldn't let her leave.

For a long time I haven't been able to eat, she said when I returned.

And then she told me that at first she hadn't wanted to, an evacuation. But soon she couldn't. Could not make herself swallow. And after a while it seemed okay. She didn't mind not eating and she walked around with bare feet. Took her shoes off and left them off so she could feel the earth below— the dark mineral-rich earth. She'd wanted to take her nourishment like a plant. She'd stand in the sun and imagine herself a tree. No, this time she'd wanted to be a bush, a bush, a vine, a tomato vine. Those spread fast, she said, and are healthy. They give off beautiful round red fruit full of viscous moistness and seed.

At that time I hadn't yet seen, blind on purpose, perhaps. But then a neighbor found her in her nightgown wandering barefoot near midnight, screaming with the peacocks in Holland Park, creeping shadow in the dark, and he coaxed her over and led her home to me. Of course I was forced to see. It was written all over her. She was ill. Had made herself sick with no food and no sleep, she shrieked then. I reached out to calm her, took her from his arms and led her to the room where I now kept her, that room without sun or earth, and fed her broth until she spat up.

I wiped her face like a baby's.

She stared into my eyes as I wiped and when I let go her face she once again began to speak: I would have loved her, she said. We would have laughed and played and sung. We would have been happy, us three. We would have run around in the sun—the dark earth. We would have gone to rivers and swum and caked ourselves in mud.

But now she was sick, she said. Like once before she had been sick. And because of this illness, the last time it had come, she had felt the need to run and leave all that was past and full of sickness behind. But she had made the mistake of leaving her daughter, from whom now she had always been gone. And the illness had come back to haunt.

She looked at me as I picked up the tray, grabbed the key to let myself out. Your face, she said, staring at me as I stood in the doorway from where she lay in bed. Your skin is so smooth, soft brown, beautiful. Your mouth a red berry—always moist—almond shaped burnt chestnut colored eyes. Her face is just like yours, she said. I've seen it.

I see it every night.

I would have adored her, she said. And both of us would have loved you too. And every time I kiss you it's a kiss that's meant for two, she said.

I'm rotten inside, she said.

I stopped reading and had to calm my breath, close my eyes.

The seat next to me had remained empty yet I felt someone stroke my hair.

I didn't open my eyes, for I knew no one was there.

I then felt deep inside the words as they were written in her letter: I'm sorry.

I know, I say in a hushed whisper.

I turn and look out the window of that plane and focus on the patchwork of browns and greens far down below me: 35,000 feet. I imagine my father in the middle of one of those fields, the green stretching out long around him. Eduardo, the baker. My father.

And then I imagine myself in that green too. I run up to him, rush gasping toward him. And then I see Manuel in his scuffed up Vans, and my mother in her paisley dress, and I reach my arms out to them.